A HELLION HARLOT NOVELLA

WRITTEN & ILLUSTRATED BY

NIKKITA BELL

THE HELLION HARLOT COLLECTION

BY NIKKITA BELL

For those haunted by their past—fear is just another thing to burn. So light the match.

That's what the Devil's Second would do.

————

And to my personal chaos demon—thank you for loving the ugly parts of me while celebrating the prettier ones.

And to those who missed our favorite evil witch.
This one's for you.

You are now entering the world of October Winters and the Hellion Harlot series.

Please be advised that this is a dark adult novella and may include themes that are disturbing to some readers.

I created this series to provide a fresh perspective on villainy, featuring bad gals you can't help but root for. It is important to remember that **this book is told from the perspective of a morally corrupt supernatural creature** who should not be held accountable to the same moral standards as a human. While I invite you to explore these darker sides, the health, safety, and mental and emotional well-being of my readers is of utmost importance to me. Please make sure to read through this list of trigger warnings to help you make an informed decision before delving into this universe.

WARNINGS: Adult language, sexual content (18+ only), depictions and references of death/murder, religious/Satanic references, body horror/demonic transformations, parental selfishness/narcissism, emotional abandonment, self-preservation over familial welfare, descriptive gore and violence, PTSD, threesome, blood play, breath play, light BDSM, nonconsensual voyeurism.

TRACK LIST

SCAN TO LISTEN TO
THE PLAYLIST HERE!

DEMONIC HIERARCHY

OF THE HELLION HARLOT SERIES

THE KING OF DEMONS

LUCIFER MORNINGSTAR / SATAN / THE DEVIL

THE THIRTEEN PRIME EVILS

HEAD DEMONS CREATED BY THE DEVIL WHO HAVE DOMINION OVER HUMANS AND SUPERNATURALS CREATURES.

DEMON OF CHAOS

DEMON OF DEBAUCHERY (CURRENTLY INHABITING LOS ANGELES, CA)

DEMON OF DECEPTION (CURRENTLY INHABITING LAS VEGAS, NV)

DEMON OF DESTRUCTION

DEMON OF DOMINATION

DEMON OF DOUBT

DEMON OF ENVY

DEMON OF GREED (CURRENTLY INHABITING MANHATTAN, NY)

DEMON OF MISFORTUNE

DEMONS OF NIGHTMARES AND FEAR (TWO-HEADED TWINS)

DEMON OF PESTILENCE (LOCATION UNKNOWN)

DEMON OF VENGEANCE

DEMON OF VIOLENCE

UNDERLINGS

HIGH-LEVEL DEMONS

MID-LEVEL DEMONS

LOWER-LEVEL DEMONS

HELLSPAWN

FOR MORE INFORMATION ON THE PRIMES, PLEASE TURN TO PG 225 FOR THE GLOSSARY

AUTHOR'S NOTE

When we last saw October Winters, she made her glorious—if ill-timed—return to the Hellion Harlot universe at the close of *To Hell with Bad Decisions.*

> *A quick note before we go further: <u>this novella is intended to be read after</u>* <u>To Hell with Bad Decisions.</u> *If you haven't read Book 2 yet, please do. Some parts of this novella will feel disjointed and will spoil you without it.*

Many of you have asked why her arc took the turn it did, where she was during the events of *Bad Decisions,* and whether we'd ever see her behind the narrator's wheel again. This novella exists to answer those questions—but it isn't a standalone story with a clean, linear journey. Think of it as a parallel thread woven through the greater Hellion Harlot timeline: a smaller piece of a much bigger puzzle.

I Hate Dead People (Too) will give you your October fix, yes—but it will also pull back the curtain on the Hellion world and its demonic hierarchy in ways the main series hasn't had the space to explore yet. Consider it the connective tissue between Books 2, 3, and 4.

Welcome to Hell, Hellions. Enjoy your stay.

NOVEMBER 1, 2003

TRACK ONE
SAD BUT TRUE

IF YOU'RE GOING TO KILL ME, JUST FUCKING DO IT ALREADY!

I'M TRYING TO. YOU'RE THE ONE REFUSING TO DIE.

FUCK ME, I'M GOING TO HELL.

TRACK ONE

SAD BUT TRUE

"COME ON, FUCKER. JUST DIE ALREADY."

My victim flails around like a damn inflatable tube man, screams echoing off of boulders and cell towers. He's an idiot, of course—no one can hear him, not all the way up this mountain. A murder of dead, decrepit crows swirls around him, picking and pulling. They're vicious little shits when freshly reanimated, tearing at his obviously fake Armani suit, yanking at the last few strands of hair on his head. "You know, Mr. Whatever-your-name-is, if you'd just hold still, this'll be over lick-ety-split."

I curl my fingers inward, channeling my death magic through dark, shadowy tendrils to force the man to his knees. His bones crack sickeningly when they hit the ground, and the zombie crows close in on him.

"If you're—*fuck*—if you're going to kill me, just

fucking do it already!" he screeches through the pain, tears streaming down his face.

"I'm trying to. You're the one refusing to die." I lie on the hood of my Camaro, resting my feet on the bumper while taking a bite of pineapple pizza, savoring both the cheese and his desperation. "Though, I will say, torturing you is *incredibly* entertaining." After the past week I've had, I'd say I've earned the right to revel in the long, drawn-out art of murder and mayhem.

He stares at me with that incredulous look—the same one he gave me when I found him, wandering Hollywood Boulevard with a bloody neck, screaming some bullshit about a vampire stripper. And judging by the ever-growing sweat on his brow, I know he's about to drop another pathetic plea.

"This can't be happening," the man mutters, trying to convince himself. "Do you want money? I've got a Roth IRA—I can pull it all out!"

"I couldn't give two shits about your money," I muse, picking a strip of ham off my pizza and taking a bite.

"Then what do you want from me?"

"Yeesh—can't a girl enjoy her celebratory slice before getting back to the grind? I just survived the ultimatum of my life; I think I've earned myself a snack and some entertainment." I clap my hands, dusting off the semolina and wiping grease on my dark jeans. "Okay, you caught me—I'm stalling. Your sacrifice is the key to opening Hell's portal, and, let me tell you, I've spent a thousand years avoiding that place. It's not exactly the stamp I've been itching for on my passport."

"But why me?" Great, the fucker thinks he can buy himself time with stupid questions. He really loves the sound of his own pitiful voice.

I shrug. "You were at the right place at the right time, and you were already bloodied up. Figured no one would miss you."

The man struggles against the shadowy tendrils of my necromancy binding his arms and legs. The acrid stench of tobacco, stale booze, and broken dreams fills the air—the delicious scent of my magic filling both our lungs. He screeches with every bite from my corpse-crows, their festering, decaying beaks far more lethal now than they ever were in life.

"This is all a bad dream," he squeaks between bird-gnaws. "That demon lady and the vampire at the motel weren't real. You're not real. Hell can't be real."

"Oh, buddy, Hell is as real as the smog choking this city. No one gets to wake up from this nightmare."

Ironic, considering nightmares are the one thing nobody's getting right now. No human or supernatural will feel that particular agony tonight. Or tomorrow. Or ever again. Not until I undo my royal fuck up and let the Demon of Nightmares and Fear back out to play.

Yet another supernatural mission on Big Bad Devil Daddy's honey-do list.

But this time, there is no impossible six-day quest, no high-stakes race against time, and certainly no demon hunters thwarting my plans.

Just me, the Devil's Second, back to reality and facing another infernal HR mess straight out of Hell's ass.

Six days ago, I rolled my punk ass back into Los Angeles, looking for a place to lie low. Instead, I ended up with a target on my head and an ultimatum that cost me everything.

Almost everything.

Mistakes were made, prices were paid, and they'll haunt me for the rest of my life—starting with the scorpion-shaped band on my left ring finger.

Its obsidian scales catch the moonlight as I hop off the car hood and saunter toward my victim. It's the perfect little thing: tiny armored body, eight legs, two pincers, and a tail curled around my finger like a promise.

Poetic justice, I call it. A life sentence for an angel who fucked with the wrong witch.

I still smell him on my jacket—overpriced cologne mixed with betrayal and heartbreak. I should burn the fucking thing, but good leather is hard to come by, and this jacket is my best accessory.

Funny how I can destroy a man and still not be free of him. My own damn fault, really.

The city sprawls out like a glittering sea below us.

It's dark up here by the Hollywood sign, but the moonlight bounces brilliantly off the gargantuan letters. The general public isn't allowed up here anymore—decades of vandalism and suicide attempts saw to that—which makes it the perfect place to hide a portal to the Underworld.

That's right. One of Hell's many portals is located at the Hollywood sign. Cherry's brilliant idea. Go fucking figure.

Believe it or not, it isn't the easiest place to access. Humans think all it takes is one sin, one dirty deed to damn your soul, but it's a lot more complicated than that. Blood sacrifice, incantations, a little smoke and mirrors—you've got to put on a show. The Devil loves theatrical flair. Fuck, all his demons do.

Sure, I've got special privileges, being his Second and all, but even those at the top of the food chain have to pay the toll.

It starts with my favorite little shape: a pentagram. I drag my heavy black boot through the soft earth. Diagonal, up. Diagonal, down. Diagonal, up. Straight across. Diagonal, down. Circle.

Then, I pull the spare crystals from the trunk of my Camaro—black kyanite and clear quartz amp up this ritual. I haul them over to each point of the star, the jagged bastards heavy as fucking watermelons. It's a miracle they didn't knock my victim unconscious while he was zip-tied in the trunk. He screamed his lungs out on our joyride up the hill after I found him wandering aimlessly around Bad Decisions. The scratches on his face suggest they got a few good hits in, though that could just be my corpse-crows having a little fun.

Either way, this asshole refuses to die, and I'm really hoping he's got some fight left in him. Spilling his blood is about to tear open the most dangerous fucking portal in existence.

"Alright, buddy." I crouch to his eye level, flashing him a sadistic grin. "Playtime's over, and I've got a date with the Devil."

Mustering whatever unholy strength is left in me, I grasp him by the collar and push him into the circle. He struggles against my grip, tugging at his tie to yield him some air. I throw him in the middle of the circle and reach into my jacket to pull out my athame, an unholy dagger gifted to me by Lucifer himself. This trusty little blade has always served me well, summoning any of the Big Thirteen at my command—or even their father. My victim catches his reflection in the steel, and his eyes widen in terror.

"No! No, no, no—"

"Shut the fuck up," I groan, rolling my eyes. "You humans are so consumed with begging and pleading and fearing death when, honestly? The mortal realm is *far* more terrifying than death itself."

The hypocrisy practically oozes from my pores. I've spent a thousand years avoiding death—well, avoiding

Hell specifically. The whole point of that damn ultimatum was ensuring I didn't end up rotting there for eternity. Eternal damnation and indentured servitude wouldn't look good on me, especially somewhere as hot as Satan's asshole.

If I wanted that, I would've stayed in Florida.

But I digress.

"I'm sure you'll find a nice little home down there, maybe with Greed or Deception. They're desperate enough to take another slug into their ranks."

Yanking the man's head back, I slice into his neck without hesitation. His screams cut to nothing as his throat rips open beneath my blade, muscle and tissue slicing like butter. The sound of his gurgling against the chirping crickets and distant city noise mixes in a twisted lullaby. He slumps to the ground as his life spills down his suit and onto the earth, painting my pentagram crimson as the crystals hum with awakened power.

All I need now are the words.

"By spilled blood of ill intent,

Of corruption and innocence well spent,

Open the gate where evil dwells,

Grant me access to the depths of Hell."

A ring of Hellfire erupts around me, the heat kissing my skin like a long-lost lover. Beneath me, the ground quakes—as it always does when the portal opens—but my feet remain planted. My victim continues bleeding out before me, his life ebbing away by the second, when a blinding light erupts from the *H* of the famous landmark.

Right in the middle, within the aperture of the letter, a fiery portal tears open. The stench of sulfur hits me like a physical blow, nearly sending bile up my throat.

God, I fucking hate that smell.

I smile down at the man at my feet, kicking his back to make him face-plant into the dirt.

"Bon voyage, slimeball." I salute the corpse as it goes limp in the center of my ritual circle.

I walk through the flames, shivering with delight as the heat envelops me without burning my clothes or skin. The portal sits frustratingly far away on top of a mound of dirt, but something catches my eye as I trudge toward the sign.

A staircase materializes, leading straight toward the portal.

The Devil thinks of everything.

Looking over my shoulder, I cast a longing glance at my Camaro. No one will find her up here, and if they do, she knows how to disappear. Powering her with a human soul was one of my more brilliant ideas, and nothing's more loyal than a possessed car brought to life with necromancy.

Hell, she's more reliable than my own familiar is now. What a sad, pitiful truth—a hunk of metal from a Nevada junkyard feels more loyal than someone who promised me forever, more loyal than even a creature soul-bound to me, a man who turned his back on me so quickly.

I shake off the thought, pushing away the bitter memories trying to drag me under.

As I begin to climb the steps, light catches in my peripheral vision. I spin around to see the corpse glowing with ethereal energy. Within seconds, his soul tears free from his body, materializing as a ghostly echo of his corporeal form before drifting skyward.

"Oh, no you don't," I mutter as his spirit begins its ascent. My fingers curl inward, and the soul tears from its heavenly path, sucking straight into my waiting palm. Mr. What's-his-face's ethereal scream fills my ears like a symphony—beautiful, agonized, and absolutely perfect.

The spirit condenses into a glowing orb, swirling with ghostly mist. I study the flickering light, and a slow smile spreads across my face. This bastard had no business going Upstairs anyway. His soul is exactly what the Devil ordered.

Instinctively, I reach for the scorpion ring around my finger to awaken Nero. But the weight of the truth hits me like a physical blow: the creature wrapped around my finger isn't my beloved familiar anymore.

It's Declan Lovejoy—the bastard who chose Heaven over me. He learned the hard way what happens when you betray the most powerful dark witch in the world.

No matter. I'll deliver this one to the Devil personally.

I suck in a deep breath as I reach the top of the stairs, skin prickling despite the warmth of my leather jacket. It isn't the biting November air or the high-altitude sending ice through my veins—it's the unyielding dread seeping into my bones as the cruel truth grows clearer with every step:

Fuck me, I'm going to Hell.

Can't say I'm surprised, though—not after spending a millennium perfecting the art of villainy. But the alternative requires a halo, and those pesky things would cramp my style. Besides, there's only one angelic accessory I'll wear for the rest of my immortality.

And he's all asshole and no glow.

TRACK TWO
THE HAND THAT FEEDS

YOUR DIMWITS KNOW BETTER THAN TO FUCK WITH ME, BOSS.
THAT, MY DARLING, IS EXACTLY WHY THEY'LL TRY.

TRACK TWO

THE HAND THAT FEEDS

Based on a thousand years of petty gossip from my demonic cohorts, I'd imagined Hell as a torture chamber of screaming souls, stinking of fire, sulfur, and brimstone, eons of the damned clinging to life with outstretched hands like a twisted Goya, begging for salvation that would never come.

But there's none of that.

Except for the smell.

This acrid, spine-tingling stench would bring the most powerful of creatures to their knees, humbling them real fucking fast.

And I'm one deep breath away from spilling my guts onto the ancient stone floor.

Once I manage to swallow the bile, replacing the rancid taste with a dramatic pull of my freshly lit cigarette, I realize I'm standing in the middle of a massive, round platform. It's suspended in what looks like some sort of supernatural limbo—deathly quiet, unassuming, eerily still. Storm clouds and darkness surround it. Lightning crackles while thunder booms in the distance, and the only light illuminating the area is the Hellish glow of the 13 portals.

Fan-fucking-tastic. I basically entered a portal to get to more portals. There's some twisted, demonic irony in there somewhere.

Expansive Gothic archways tower in a perfect circle, mimicking a clock face that rivals the elegance of a cathedral window. Roman numerals mark each threshold, accompanied by Hellspeak inscriptions. They twist like a child's scribbles, marking each of the Prime Evils.

Greed. Deception. Debauchery. Violence. Domination. Misfortune. Doubt. Envy. Vengeance. Chaos. Pestilence. Destruction. Nightmares and Fear.

So this is it. The Ring of the Thirteen.

I hate to admit it, but Hell isn't exactly what I pictured. Funny. I expected nine circles, each one more infernal than the last. Guess Dante got it all wrong.

I'd heard about this unholy phenomenon over the years, when lesser and mid-tier demons would blab about their home realms, how each one perfectly embodied the vice of their constitution. Rumor has it: The Realms are where each Prime lives and rules. However, some take vacations to the human realm to fuck with humanity, throwing in a few cataclysmic life events every now and then. Destruction and Pestilence love doing that shit every century or so. The Bubonic Plague was particularly entertaining. Vesuvius too.

The hairs on my neck stand as I firmly plant my boots on a demonic ram's head carved in black obsidian at the center of the platform. A canal cuts from the center to one of the portals—one bathed in gold and green light, bleeding corruption and deceit. I scan the archaic word carved into the arch.

Greed. Naturally.

The mechanics of this…limbo, if you can call it that, completely baffle me. What in the actual fuck is this canal for? Hell doesn't exactly come with a visitor's guide, and all I've got to go on is a thousand years of eavesdropping on demonic gossip.

Sure, I could have come better prepared—called in a few favors, done a little research—but that would require thinking past "kill things and see what happens." Not really my thing. Very unfun.

I crouch, studying the ram's head jutting from the floor. Lightning flickers above me, and I press my hand to the gaping maw, nearly jolting back as my skin sizzles.

Fuck—that shit burns worse than a UTI.

I feel the ground beneath my feet, hot and unforgiving, wondering what lies under the ancient stone platform. Is this where the Devil stores the souls I deliver? Is this where the eternal torture happens?

It all feels too quiet for my liking. Hell shouldn't be this still.

Where are the trillions of demons? Where are all the souls? Why isn't this place on fucking fire?

Curiosity tugs at my insides as I take careful steps around the platform. The rubber soles of my boots scratch against stone, my leather jacket groaning in protest as I fold my arms. I walk toward the edge and peer over.

Ah, there they all are.

At first, it looks like a sea of fire, but the longer I stare, the more I realize this platform is suspended over a literal ocean of dead souls. The Pit of the Lost—I remember reading about it in that handy little grimoire I stole from a necromancer in the 1870s. What a time that was.

But my curiosity is cut short when a sudden, familiar chill spreads through my core, a chill I know all too well.

"Hello, Toby."

I struggle to stand upright, nearly losing my balance at the platform's edge. I spin around, fighting to regain my composure as I'm faced with the most gruesome yet beautiful creature I've ever laid eyes on.

Lucifer Morningstar, the King of Demons, stands before me in his true form. A devastatingly handsome grin splits his demonic features, his arms outstretched, as if welcoming me home.

I can't help but let out a sigh of relief. "Hiya, boss."

His crimson skin almost glitters in the ambient light cast by the gates of his sons' realms. Void-like eyes search me as the corners crinkle with his growing smirk. Long, dark tendrils of curly hair fall past his shoulders, framing his beautiful face—those cutting features so sharp, they could draw blood.

"Wasted no time, I see."

I wave my hand dismissively. "It was either this or catch up on sleep, and I know you would have found a way to haunt my dreams until you put me back to work."

His deep chuckle booms as loud as the thunder above. "Look at you, prioritizing business over pleasure."

God, that couldn't be further from the truth—but I'll let him have this one.

"I trust you found your way through the portal with little complication," he begins, circling me like a predator stalking its prey.

"I'm here, aren't I?"

"As I live and breathe. Need a crash course on the Ring of the Thirteen?"

"You mean this spiky demonic asshole?" I gesture at the arches and the demonic maw in the center, which probably looks exactly like my colorful description from an aerial view.

The ground trembles beneath us with Lucifer's

growing displeasure, his brows drawing together as his wings unfurl to span ten feet. "Mind your cheek, Toby. You're in my world now."

I straighten my posture and drop my arms to my sides. Flashing him a sardonic smile, I curtsy. "Honored to be here, my liege."

Lucifer ignores my sarcasm. "You remember why you're here, of course."

My voice is as bland as boiled chicken, like a child reciting her times tables. "Break the curse of banishment on Nightmares and Fear. Restore their access to the human realm so they can resume mind-fucking mortals and feeding on their terror. Balance of good and evil, yadda-yadda."

"Careful, my rotten one. That sharp tongue and callousness earned you enough enemies down here to wage a war. Before you begin your work, there are some ground rules you must follow." He steps behind me, and suddenly, this endless chasm feels a little too small. "You require permission from the respective Prime to enter their realm. Blood sacrifice unlocks their gate, and only then will you gain access. You are not, under any circumstances, permitted to harm any demon whilst inside their realm. That is their territory, and unless you want to give my sons another reason to rip this beautiful head from your neck, I suggest you abide by that rule. Understood?"

His ground rules only stir more questions. "'*Permis-*

sion?' You mean I can't just waltz inside the Nightmare and Fear Realm and have a nice ol' chat with the terror twins?"

"You thought it would be that easy?" His laugh is cold. "My twins despise you after what you did to them. You're persona non grata in their domain."

"Then how am I supposed to break their curse? I need to enter their realm and perform an unbinding ritual, and I can't do that from out here."

His dark features soften as he studies me. "I've taken the liberty of making some arrangements for you. Before you can enter the Ninth Realm, you must stop at the Eighth first." He nods toward the arch labeled VIII—the one surrounded by a swarm of bees.

My eyes immediately dart to the arch just left of the Nightmare and Fear gate. Everything about it makes my stomach lurch, from the Hellspeak inscription above to the mindfuck of the portal itself.

"E-eighth?" I can't quite mask the anxiety bleeding through my frustration.

"Indeed." His lips curl in a devious smile. "I have a gift waiting for you there."

That underlying playfulness tells me whatever he's planning is the exact fucking opposite of a gift.

"I don't like the way you said that, boss. Nothing good comes out of Eight."

"Nothing good comes out of any of the Thirteen." Lucifer's dark, imposing shadow looms over me. My eyes shut instinctively as he runs his strong hands up my shoulders. It's like I can feel his skin against mine through the thickness of my leather jacket, tracing every nerve in my body and setting them ablaze. "Trust me, my rotten one—you'll thank me later."

I'm temporarily mesmerized by our shadows—how his long horns curve upward and inward like a predator's crown, how his wings flex and shudder with every chuckle that rumbles through his chest. After a while, I can't see myself anymore. His darkness swallows me whole, and I let it. It's all his. It's always fucking his.

"And Toby." The Devil's gravelly voice slithers up my spine as his fingers trail along my shoulder. "Do play nice with my sons while you're down here. You've got time to make up for, and I just got you back." His grip tightens. "It would be such a waste to lose you so soon."

My breath hitches as I feel his lips press against my neck, hot breath searing my skin. I fight the shiver with a shrug and force out a chuckle. "Your dimwits know better than to fuck with me, boss."

"That, my darling"—his voice drops to a dangerous whisper— "is *exactly* why they'll try." His fingers slide down my shoulder to my hips, pulling me flush against him. "You'll come visit me before heading back up, won't you, Toby?"

"Not if you keep calling me that."

His tongue clicks in that patronizing way, voice

dropping to pure, condescending sadist. "Oh, come now. Surely you'll let me have my fun. It's been too long."

"One year, Luci. One fucking year I was gone. You're starting to sound like a lovesick teenager. Real attractive for the King of Demons."

"A year on the human plane is a lifetime down here, dear. That's a lifetime spent missing that pretty little cu—"

"Nope. Don't you dare try to distract me with the sex talk. You want me to do your dirty work, and that's that." I wriggle against his grasp, and for a moment, I wonder who's really in charge here. Then, his voice drops to ice, and I remember.

"*My* dirty work?" He gives my hips a punishing squeeze before releasing me. "Need I remind you it was *your* poor judgment that landed you in this mess to begin with?"

I can't form a response, no matter how hard I try. No witty one-liners, no defensive retorts. He's right. Too fucking right. But despite the intimidation in his voice, he still looks at me like I'm precious—just like he did when I first came into his service. "I sure do enjoy the mess you've become, my rotten one."

I twist my lips into a mockery of a smile. "All the better to entertain you with, my liege."

"The maw is the blood sacrifice vessel," he says, gesturing at the obsidian ram on the floor. "Spill yours and speak the name of the Prime whose realm you wish to enter. If you have permission, you can go. Don't worry—he's expecting you." He pauses, cupping my cheek with his large hand, fingers curling in my short blonde hair. "Enjoy your stay, Toby. Break the curse on my twins, or our next reunion will be far less pleasant than this one."

"Wait—" I call out before he disappears into the darkness. "No impossible deadline? No stakes? No ultimatum?"

A devious smile cracks his features, and he spreads his arms and wings wide, drawing my attention to the clock face of portals surrounding us. "I told you. Time works differently Downstairs. The question isn't when you'll finish—it's whether your soul will still be intact when you do."

The King of Demons steps onto the obsidian ram's head and explodes into Hellfire, vanishing in a blaze of light and leaving me alone, dread and frustration burning under my skin.

Lucifer's command rings in my head on repeat as I scan the arches. Each one reflects its dominion through color, elements, symbols, or sounds. Pestilence's gate sends an unwelcome shiver up my spine. The cracked threshold seeps a sickly green miasma, surrounded by a swarm of locusts, and reeks of absolute death.

Ugh. Glad that fucker hasn't been seen in ages. No

Prime has ever made me want to gouge my eyes out more.

I spin until I finally land on number Eight. The assault on my vision makes me question the Devil's motives, and I consider diving headfirst into whatever clusterfuck awaits me in Nightmare and Fear's Realm— despite the whole not-having-permission thing.

Portal number Eight can't decide what it wants to be; the stone threshold melts into metal, cracking with wooden veins, then dissolves into water for a heartbeat before crumbling to dust. It does the whole shebang all over again, like some fucked-up magic show. Light and shadow strobe erratically from within, throwing me back to those '90s raves that would give me migraines for days. In fact, I feel one coming on right now.

The Devil and his sons have a sick, twisted sense of humor.

I reach into my jacket, fingers finding the familiar weight of my athame. Sacrifice is currency when it comes to the Underworld—always has been, always will be. My palm shows no trace of the cut from a few hours ago when I summoned him at the cemetery. Time is a weird construct, especially in Hell. I slice deep into fresh skin, feeling the blade part my flesh like silk.

Crouching beside the demonic ram's head, I ball my fist tight. My thousand-year-old blood drips into its fanged maw, thick drops hissing against obsidian. I speak the name of the Prime whose realm I seek, and the ram's eyes ignite crimson. My blood races through the canal, and the platform lurches into motion, spinning quickly with grinding stone until it stops.

Right on Eight.

I rise, slip on my aviators, and shield my eyes from the now-blazing archway. The canal stretches before me, scraped clean of blood, leading to the portal that makes my brain want to leak out of my ears, despite the shades.

"*Welcome, October Winters,*" a high-pitched, sing-song voice screeches in Hellspeak.

"Bite me," I mutter, flicking my spent cigarette into the pit of screaming souls below.

Whatever "gift" the Devil's got for me beyond that archway better be fucking worth it.

With one last breath of sanity, I close my eyes, swallow my doubts, and cross the threshold into madness itself.

The Chaos Realm.

TRACK THREE
EVERYTHING ZEN
OCTOBER FUCKING WINTERS! THE DEVIL'S SECOND, THE WITCH WHO TOLD HEAVEN TO GO FUCK ITSELF AND MEANT IT!

TRACK THREE

EVERYTHING ZEN

The visceral urge to vomit slams into me as I cross into the Eighth Realm. Traveling between worlds isn't some casual stroll—or so I've been told. It shatters the laws of physics and wreaks havoc on the body, but hey, when have physics or logic ever mattered in Hell? Some demons, depending on their constitution, don't survive the trip. I may or may not have known a few.

Fortunately, I'm no demon—and I'm too old and too high up the food chain for such bad luck. After a thousand years of dodging death, it'd be a damn shame to die from realm sickness.

Every one of my senses is overwhelmed by this fucked-up place. I remove my sunglasses to take in the place. It's like a Dalí painting fucked a Picasso and their offspring had a seizure—no form, no order, no logic. The floors and walls—or lack thereof—shift and writhe

the longer I stare. Nothing is where it belongs. Nothing stays in one spot.

Hell, this place is a surrealist's wet dream. Believe me, I ate that shit up in the '20s. No one loves bizarre more than I do. But this...

This is the culmination of every avant-garde esotericist's deepest, most depraved fantasy, the kind of place that doesn't just inspire madness.

Chaos *invented* it.

Come to think of it, this is probably what got Dalí hard in the first place. Wonder if he's down here.

Trying to follow some sense of a path, I stride forward. Hellspawn chitter and chortle as they trail behind Chaos Underlings like lost, depraved puppies. The Underlings themselves are so caught up in their own maelstrom of insanity, I might as well have stepped into an asylum for the damned.

My boot plunges into a puddle of—what even is that? Some disgusting goo. It's there one second, gone the next. I'm better off not knowing.

As I continue my trek through the weirdness that is the Chaos Realm, bees swarm overhead, the buzz assaulting my ears. I swear, one of those fuckers is going to take my eye out. Devil can't blame me for getting rid of pests, especially if they thwart my mission. I slip on my aviators again, shielding myself from any untimely assault by the pesky pollinators, and snap my fingers.

The swarm ignites in a glorious burst of my Hellfire.

There. That'll teach them to get close.

Except it doesn't. It only makes them angrier.

Nothing sets the nerves ablaze quite like actual bees on fire. I suppose undead bees are no better than mortal ones—light them up, and they just take it personally—but they've got nothing to lose down here.

The little show excites the pants off the Underlings. Some join in on the chaos, lobbing their own magic into the fray. Others sit back and laugh so maniacally, it vibrates my bones.

A growl burns in my chest.

I blast the swarm again, but this time, I don't just burn—I siphon. Their essence drains into my palms until they drop dead midair, collapsing into hundreds of tiny black orbs on the ground. Bite-sized demon souls.

Nero would lose his mind over these.

The urge to whisper his awakening spell tugs at me, the words already forming on my tongue. My fingers curl inward when the bitter reminder seeps into my mind: Nero's not here. Not anymore. And Lovejoy isn't worthy of a little demonic treat.

It's too soon. He hasn't suffered enough, frozen in time as a ring, and facing him isn't exactly at the top of my to-do list.

But an audience with the Demon of Chaos is.

As if on cue, a loud, booming voice reverberates through whatever passes for walls in this realm. I spin around...and suddenly, I'm somewhere else.

A throne room, maybe? If throne rooms were designed by a migraine.

It's like stepping inside a living kaleidoscope. Form and matter gave up here; they just quit, packed their bags, and fucked off entirely. Colors bleed into each other, fragments shifting and rearranging on an infinite loop. Some spots churn slowly and hypnotically, almost beautifully. Others spin at a pace that makes my stomach lurch.

And there it is again—the visceral urge to vomit. I hate this fucking place.

The voice returns, this time in a mismatched, frenzied laugh, like a tape being sped up and slowed down at random, sound folding over itself. I squint, trying to make out a form through the madness of color, but the sheer disorder of this place forces my eyes shut.

Pitch black envelops me.

I've never been more grateful for the darkness.

"October Winters!"

The voice is clearer now. When I open my eyes, I see him: short, stout, round as a fucking kettle, perched on a throne made entirely of living bees. His limbs make no sense for his form. *Nothing* about him makes sense.

Put Humpty Dumpty in a blender and give him a crown. That's this guy.

The Demon of Chaos tumbles off his mound of bees and waddles over to me. "October fucking Winters! The Devil's Second, the witch who told Heaven to go fuck itself and meant it!" He bounces on his stubby legs like an overexcited chihuahua. "My sweetheart—light of my life—please make yourself at home! Kick your feet up. It's been too long." His form flickers, briefly sprouting extra arms that gesture wildly. "Welcome to Hell! I hear it's your first time. Can I get'cha anything? A coffee? How 'bout the blood of the innocent? Chupacabra piss? I got a fresh batch on the stove—"

"Shut the fuck up." I pinch the bridge of my nose, the migraine finally winning. "*God*—"

"God's not here, dollface. You're on the wrong plane." His face shifts into something with too many teeth. "And speaking of planes—airports these days. What's with the shoes?"

"Nope, no." I turn toward the nearest exit. "I don't have time for this shit. I'm out of here."

"But baby, you just got here! C'mon, how does that song go?" He starts singing off tune, his voice crackling like radio static, while snapping his fingers to some beat. "It's cold outside!"

At this point, I'm ready to shove a piano down his throat.

"Lucifer said you have something for me." My voice is flat, dead.

"Guilty as charged! Well, uh, not guilty, never guilty. That would imply I follow rules." His form ripples like disturbed water. "Rules are for boring people, and you, my beautiful disaster, are not boring.

Quite the opposite! A perfect conundrum of chaos." He grins with a mouth that's suddenly too wide. "And I would know."

The little fuck is trying my patience. "Listen, bud. I've got a date at the Nightmare and Fear Realm. I'm gonna need you to stick to one train of thought before my brain melts out of my ears."

"Ah, business—always business with the Devil's Second. Never catchin' a break, you poor thing. Alright, alright." His form suddenly stills, the chaotic shifting grinding to a halt as he settles back into his short, rotund shape. His features solidify into something almost human—two eyes, four limbs, and a face that doesn't make my retinas burn.

"Thank fuck," I mutter under my breath.

"So, word on the street is, you're headed to the twins," Chaos starts.

"I just told you that."

"That's right, you did! But so did my pops. See, he thinks you're not welcome there. For what reason, I wouldn't know. How could anyone hate a pretty thing like you? You're just so nice."

My features twist into something like pure disbelief. "Are you fucking serious?"

"With you? Never." He wriggles his bushy eyebrows. "Anyways, so pops calls me up, says his witch is comin' Downstairs for the first time and needs someone to look out for her. Y'know, even on a good day, the Nightmares and Fear Realm is a fucked-up kinda place—not suitable for someone like you."

"Someone like me?"

"Yeah. All-powerful and legendary. That place is beneath you."

Finally, he's talking some sense. Still, I'd love for him to cut to the chase.

"But you see, in order to get into their realm, you need permission. An invitation. Just like the other 12, you know how it goes. And from what I gather, you're Public Enemy No. 1 over there. So, you're gonna need someone who's got security clearance. Round-the-clock access, no questions asked. Someone who can get'cha in without settin' off any alarms."

I groan. "Please tell me it's not you."

"Oh, honey, no. I've got someone way more qualified —the best of my best! Ey, Mayhem!"

The Chaos Prime waves his thick, stubby arm toward someone behind me. Within seconds, a tall, imposing figure approaches, staring at me like I'm a puzzle he's dying to take apart piece by piece.

"Mayhem, my boy! My magnum opus. C'mere, kid."

The Underling stalks toward us with predatory grace, and every hair on my body stands on end. Literally. Each blonde strand lifts beneath my sleeves as electric currents radiate off his skin. I brace for supernatural impact, but instead, an incessant buzzing fills my ears, making me cringe.

He's an unstable, erratic creature, covered neck to toe in geometric patterns that look like tattoos in this light. But as he draws closer, I realize they're scars. Dark, demonic ichor pulses beneath the raised flesh—bruised and macabre. And they're…moving, dancing across his skin like moving pictures. It would almost be beautiful, if it weren't for the unsettling vibrations rolling off him in waves.

His face cuts into a feral grin as he takes his place beside the Chaos Prime, towering over him by at least two feet. He's lithe and lean, tail flicking with serpentine grace, despite his chaotic nature. I swallow hard when I finally meet his gaze.

His face is split in half. On one side, a monstrous maw of massive, sharp teeth and exposed muscle highlights a void-like eye rimmed with teeth that curl outward like claws. The other half stretches into an almost normal smile, but that eye…

That eye is pure madness.

It's a kaleidoscope, an actual fucking kaleidoscope spinning hypnotically, filled with every color imaginable as it studies me with predatory interest.

"What in the actual—" The words die in my throat.

"October Winters, meet Mayhem, First of Chaos."

A First. The equivalent of the Devil's Second to any Prime. Whatever this creature did to earn his position, it must have been spectacular. I can respect that.

Almost.

"Pleasure to finally meet you," the Underling speaks, his voice as disturbing as his appearance. It's like an old gramophone clinging to life, desperate to wheeze out the last of its warped music before it dies completely.

I force a smile that probably looks more like a pained grimace. "Wish I could say the same."

The Chaos Prime beams, looking at us both excitedly. "Mayhem here's got access to every realm, and he's got friends in high *and* low places. He'll get you out of any pinch—a real charmer, my boy. Could sell bark to a tree if he wanted."

"It's tough to say no to someone with my particular gifts." Mayhem's voice shifts, clearer now, but fractured —like three versions of him speaking at once, not quite in sync. That unsettling smile widens, showing more of those monstrous teeth.

I *really* don't want to know what those gifts are.

"He's all yours until you don't need him anymore, doll." Chaos pushes his First toward me with a paternal pride that's deeply unsettling. Mayhem's tail twitches with barely contained excitement as he looms before me. "Just bring him back in one piece, will ya? He's my favorite—my top earner. Did you know he single-handedly stocked Bedlam with their finest specimens? Oh, and that King George…" He chuckles, the sound like grinding gears. "It was a hoot watching that one talk to furniture, wasn't it, kid?"

Mayhem's kaleidoscope eye spins faster, and that

grin stretches wider. "His Majesty had such creative conversations with his chair."

Any normal person would be horrified at the revelation, but I'm just deranged enough to see the merit in this…Mayhem. I mask my intrigue with an indifferent shrug and a forced, monotonous drawl. "Lovely—a Chaos demon with a résumé."

"Not as impressive or extensive as yours, of course." Mayhem regards me with those peculiar, mismatched eyes, and there's something in his voice that almost sounds like respect.

"Alright, kids, get yourselves outta here before the walls turn into water and flood the place." The Chaos Prime ushers us toward his portal with surprising urgency.

"Still haven't gotten that fixed, boss?" Mayhem's chuckle sends ice shooting up my spine.

"Your brothers and sisters have been at it for centuries—everything they touch turns to water! Can't keep a damn wall solid for more than an hour!"

I shake my head, pinching the bridge of my nose. "Fucking idiots."

"Happy trails, you two." The Prime slaps us both on the back, and the force sends us rocketing through the hexagonal barrier before I can tell him to go fuck himself.

Realm sickness hits the moment we step out of the portal—bile rising, knees threatening to buckle. Mayhem's laugh fills my ears, and, in seconds, his long, spindly fingers splay across the exposed skin of my abdomen.

The urge to vomit vanishes and manifests as a ball of green, festering energy in his hands.

"What the fuck is that?"

"This would have been your vomit." He rolls the pulsing mass between his palms like a toy. "It's Pit garbage now."

He tosses it over his shoulder. I lean over the edge of the platform, watching the ball plummet into the chasm below. Heat rises in waves, carrying with it a sound I'll never get used to: thousands—maybe millions—of voices tangled together, wailing, pleading, screaming from the Pit of the Lost.

The unclaimed. The forgotten. Souls who never found purpose, doomed to wander for eternity in a sea of fire and regret.

And I put most of them there.

Their woes wash over me, louder than any spirit on the human plane. Some have been trapped here longer than I've been alive, while some are brand new, likely fresh off a reaping from one of the Devil's low-ranking agents.

The only regret I have is not sending them all here myself. Maybe then, they'd rename it the Pit of Winters. Then again, the only pit I care about is one with a good band and a crowd that hits back.

"How did you do that?" I ask, straightening myself.

Mayhem drapes himself against arch number Eight, all languid limbs and sharp angles. "Just one of my niftier tricks. Chaos magic bends physiology. I can manifest your emotions into whatever physical form I want." He grins, all teeth. "What happens after is dealer's choice."

"Nifty," I repeat. "What'll it cost to get your boss to teach me that?"

That twisted grin only grows. "Maybe if you sidle up to his First, get on his good side…" He tilts his head, eye glinting. "I'll put in a good word."

I shrug. "I've fucked uglier demons for less."

"Aw, you think I'm ugly?" He feigns offense, bottom lip jutting out, that peculiar kaleidoscope eye spinning slower now. It's fucking *weird*.

"You're definitely…hard to look at."

My choice of words stirs something in him.

A thoughtful hum rumbles through his chest. He pushes off the arch and stalks closer, movements too fluid for something so disordered. His whole ensemble screams "Chaos demon"—nothing matches, everything clashes, yet somehow, he pulls it off with an unsettling confidence that makes it work.

The top half of his attire is straight out of those goth clubs I frequented in the '80s—sheer fishnet shirt, cropped leather jacket—while his bottom half looks like black tactical gear paired with ankle-high combat boots. The black leather gloves covering his unnaturally long fingers are cut off mid-palm, like they're one size too small.

"Do I make you uncomfortable, baby?" Both eyes lock onto mine—the black one almost worse somehow, because it makes the spinning chaos of the other more jarring.

"What is this, Olympic tryouts for uncomfortable eye contact?" I hold my ground, fighting the shiver crawling up my spine. "Stare at something else, creep."

The demon scoffs, but his gaze doesn't waver. "The Chaos Broodline won the gold for discomfort centuries ago, y'know. It's our claim to fame." He tilts his head, kaleidoscope eye spinning lazily. "I'm just deciding which parts of you I want to keep." His eye spins faster as it trails from my face to my chest. "Your heart does pretty, pretty things when you're annoyed. I'd love to see what it does when I get you hot and bothered."

I blink. "Did you just threaten to harvest my organs *and* hit on me in the same breath?"

"Maybe." He laughs, low and delighted. "Did it work?"

"I'll give you points for audacity, but you're losing them fast." I cross my arms. "Next you'll tell me you were the mastermind behind every American serial killer."

"American *and* European." He grins proudly, forked tongue poking through his demonic teeth. "And don't play coy with me, baby. We both know you've got a bigger body count than I do."

I shoot him a look. "One more comment, and I'm adding you to that body count—and not the one you're hoping for."

He rocks back on his heels, unbothered. "Jeez, you sure are rough around the edges. Who the fuck hurt you?"

"I've got a thousand years of bullshit behind me and zero time to unpack it all. Especially not with you."

"Only a thousand?" He lets out a low whistle. "You look fantastic for your age. I wouldn't peg you for a day over 850." He pauses, that insufferable smirk returning. "Now, if you wanted to peg *me*—different conversation. Totally on the table, though."

I ignore him, conjuring my stolen grimoire into my waiting hands, flipping the pages for whatever notes I scribbled down from the rumors I heard about the demonic realms. This was back when I still thought I'd remember things forever. A thousand years has a way of proving you wrong. It's a wonder I can still remember the Washington administration.

Sadly, past-October wasn't smart enough to write much about Nightmares and Fear. Probably because they fucking suck and I avoid them like the plague.

Mayhem steps into my personal bubble behind me, and my patience wears thin. A mixture of my fire and death magic builds, fighting for dominance, clawing up my chest like two animals trapped in the same rib cage.

"Ah, c'mon, Winters. Give me something to work with." His sing-song voice taunts me. "Whaddya got? I mean, it's no secret you're fucking the big boss. That's got daddy issues written all over it. But nah, there's something more—betrayed by a lover?" His creepy eyes snag on my hand. "Nice ring, by the way. Is that vintage?"

I slam my grimoire shut and spin around to face him, teeth clenched. "Can it, fuckface, or I'll split you in two and turn you into a pair of earrings."

"Ooh, hit a nerve." His forked tongue licks his lips again. "Let me guess…ex-boyfriend? Girlfriend? Someone tried to 'fix you,' and you put them in the ground?"

Irritation builds until it reaches its peak, and the death magic wins out. My hand collides with his chest, and I shove a pulse of raw, necromantic energy straight into him. Not enough to kill him, no—but enough to make him think twice before trying that shit again.

The demon staggers, knees buckling and body wriggling as my magic consumes him.

And then, he moans.

"Oh, *fuck* yes." His maniacal laugh echoes throughout the expanse while he clutches his sternum. "Do that again."

"You're sick."

"And you are fucking *spectacular*." He straightens, rolling his shoulders like I just gave him the greatest massage of his life. "I'm going to have *so* much fun with you."

"Sadist," I mutter under my breath.

"Masochist, actually," he corrects cheerfully. "But I'll give you points for audacity, October Winters."

The temperature around us spikes—so fast, so intense, I'm certain I set something off by accident. But there are no flames. Not from me. Not from anyone.

The platform itself is burning.

The rubber soles of my boots start to melt, fusing to the stone, anchoring me in place. I tug forward, trying to wrench them free.

"Please tell me you're not a pyromaniac Chaos demon," I grit through my teeth, soles sinking deeper with every second.

"No pyro. Just maniac." Mayhem drops into a crouch, palm flat against the stone. His face shifts into something I haven't seen on him yet—concern.

"Ah, shit."

Before I can ask, the platform shudders, and not like it did when I accessed the Chaos Realm. This is deeper, heavier—like something beneath us is waking up. Growing. Rising.

Wailing from the Pit swells, no longer ambient or distant.

Desperate. Hungry. Aimed.

Ah, shit is right.

They start to crawl up from the edge of the platform by the hundreds, translucent forms writhing in Hellfire, dragging themselves over the lip of stone like the damned clawing from a grave.

Their flames don't just burn—they devour. Wherever spectral fire touches the platform, the stone blackens and cracks, ancient ground sizzling into nothing.

The ambient light from the 13 arches flickers. Then, the entire platform plunges into darkness, save for the glow of the spirits themselves. Hundreds of burning, broken things pull themselves across the ground.

Their spectral eyes find me.

Every single one of them.

Hands outstretched, fingers bent and grasping.

Mouths open in silent screams that rattle my core and pierce my brain.

Something warm drips across my lip. My fingers find my nose, and it comes back slick.

Blood. Fucking great.

"October Winters." My name spreads like wildfire across thousands of ethereal lips, hissing, snarling.

"Fans of yours?" Mayhem asks as we stagger toward

the center of the platform. My boots squelch with every step, soles half-melted into the stone.

Their heat seeps through what's left of the rubber, licking at my feet, and I smirk.

Stupid dead people. Fire can't hurt a witch—it's the same fire I wield in my veins.

I kick off my ruined boots without breaking stride.

"Something like that."

Barefoot, I step through the melted rubber footprints and plant myself in front of Mayhem, fingers splayed, necromantic magic pulsing through me like a second heartbeat.

If they want a fight, I'll give them one. I put most of them here, but I have no intention of joining them.

TRACK FOUR
PEOPLE = SHIT
YOU DON'T EVEN RECOGNIZE ME, DO YOU?
BET YOU'D REMEMBER ME IF WE WERE BACK ON THAT STAGE, WITH THE DEVIL INSIDE ME.

TRACK FOUR

PEOPLE = SHIT

WHY IS IT THAT ANY TIME I'M SENT TO DO THE UNHOLY Lord's dirty work, dead people have the nerve to spoil all my fun?

Thousands—no, tens of thousands—of dead souls surround us, their spectral forms frozen in the condition their bodies held at death. Some appear old and withered while others are mangled from accidents or brutal murders—severed limbs, burned skin, the works. A few are barely clinging to human form, more shadow than spirit.

But every single one of them wants me dead, even the ones I didn't personally send here.

"Haven't seen this many in a hot minute," Mayhem's voice carries a manic edge as he rubs his hands together. "You put 'em all here?"

"More than half, give or take. I don't exactly keep

track. I assume the rest probably just hate me by association. I'm one lucky gal."

"Beautiful, deadly, *and* modest? You really are perfect."

We back toward the platform's center, nearly stumbling over the obsidian ram's head jutting from the stone. "Get behind me," I bark, shoving him against my side. "You take the southeast and southwest quadrants; I'll handle the north. Get rid of them—whatever it takes."

"You've never fought lost souls before, have you, babe?" His voice carries dark amusement even as spirits close in from all sides.

"I've never been down here before, so no." A soul swipes at my face, its translucent hand missing by inches. "What's the difference?"

"Down here, they're supercharged—stronger, faster, meaner than anything topside." I can practically hear the grin in his voice as electricity begins crackling behind me. "But don't worry, beautiful. I've got your back. Let's paint this fucking Ring red. Or blue. Or green. Whatever color ectoplasm is."

Two against a bajillion, Mayhem and I launch into battle. I start by siphoning souls into my palm, wishing my familiar were awake to suck them into his stinger. But I don't have time for a reunion with Lovejoy's vindictive ass right now. Knowing him, he'd probably refuse to help and tell me to go fuck myself.

I channel the siphoned souls, transforming them into a sphere of pure necromantic energy before hurling it toward the endless horde. The blast tears through dozens of spirits, scattering them like smoke, but they're just a fraction of those closing in on me now.

They swarm me in seconds, spectral hands clawing at my clothes and yanking my hair, threatening to rip me apart, piece by piece. I snarl against their assault, channeling raw magic through each translucent form until they collapse into writhing balls of shadow at my feet.

I feel the baby hairs at my nape curl into tight spirals as sweat pools around my collar. It sticks to my skin in that irritating way that makes me want to throw my hair into a messy bun and hurl this leather jacket off the fucking platform. Christ, it's sweltering down here. Leather definitely wasn't designed for infernal combat.

I'm not one to shy away from a fight as long as I've exhausted all my other options. Who am I kidding—I'm one of the laziest bitches in the entire universe. I already raised the dead to reap 700 souls at a concert. I'd do just about anything to get rid of these dead fucks without lifting a finger.

Specifically, to take advantage of a horny-ass demon who'd do just about anything to win my approval.

I glance back at Mayhem, catching glimpses of his chaos magic disintegrating souls by the handful, when a brilliant idea strikes me.

The quickest way to get rid of them would be to hurtle them headfirst through the 13 portals. It would all be over in an instant. If only I could open them myself.

"Mayhem!" I shout as I blast a cluster of spirits away with my necromancy. "Open the gates! Any of them— all of them!"

"You fucking nuts?" he screeches, hurling two unnaturally large, howling spirits off the platform's edge. "If I crack those portals open, they'll swarm inside! You don't need enemies in *every* realm, babe!"

"I'll take my chances!" I duck under a spirit's clawing grasp, spinning to face three more converging from different angles. "Just pick the least important one!"

"We don't play favorites down here. They're all important—" His words cut off when a shrieking corpse latches onto his shoulder from behind. As he releases a monstrous, demonic snarl, Mayhem's jaw unhinges as his neck twists like an owl to completely devour the spirit's ethereal head as it disintegrates. Electric currents arc from his gruesome maw, crackling like lightning between each razor-sharp tooth as he thrums with raw energy. "Don't fucking touch me, you dead fucks." His voice drops to something low and inhuman, like a machine learning to growl.

Despite the mayhem—both literal and demonic—I fight the shocking grin tugging at my lips. It's like watching a male demonic version of myself devour a threat. No remorse, no hesitation, just raw, unfiltered power and a snippy comeback when the dust settles.

It's like looking in a fucking mirror.

It's impressive. *He's* impressive. But I wouldn't be in this mess if he'd just kept his damn mouth shut.

My admiration is cut short when the onslaught grinds to a halt.

The dead turn their heads toward another spirit parting through their masses. A teal blue outline blazes stark against their reds and oranges, like a neon sign announcing my doom. This spirit moves with deliberate slowness, her tall, muscular frame dragging, as if her own limbs can barely support her weight. I've seen it countless times before in graveyards: this one is weighed down by the grief of death—literally.

Spectral chains only form when a spirit clings to the mortal world before descending here. She didn't want to die, but her grief wasn't strong enough to make her a ghost, instead tethering her to the human plane.

The chains hang from her glowing form, wrapped tight around her neck and wrists, and I tilt my head at the sight. She's fresh—newly freed from the manacles that bound her when she was delivered to Hell.

The question is: did I send her here? Or did someone else do the honors?

"October Winters?" The spirit's voice is gravelly and haunting.

"She can't come to the phone right now. Leave a message after the beep."

Apparently, spirits don't have a sense of humor. This one hisses at my sarcasm, lunging forward until her hands wrap around my throat. She's faster than any ordinary spirit I've faced in the mortal realm—as if Hell has supercharged her power, just like Mayhem suggested. Eerie white tendrils of spiritual energy spill from her ghostly form like liquid smoke. The weight of her chains dangles over me as she pins me to the ground, fingernails digging into my neck. But instead of physical pain, I feel something else—spiritual magic coursing through her touch.

Death magic. Magic just like mine.

"Should've stayed off my stage, you murdering bitch." Her growl echoes like something straight out of my worst nightmare. "I'm gonna make you bleed for every goddamn life you stole."

The army of spirits closes in around us, and I'm running out of time. I may not have faced a horde like this before, but I sure as fuck am not about to let a bunch of dead people overpower me. I wriggle beneath her grasp, my own voice coming out raspy and strained as my fingers begin channeling death magic. "Oh, honey, get in l-line. If you think you're the first soul I've reaped with a vendetta against me, you've got another thing c-coming."

"You don't even recognize me, do you?" The spirit's

hollow eyes shift from white to black. For a moment, there's something almost human about her. Familiar, maybe. But this charred, gothic nightmare doesn't ring a single fucking bell.

Still, the chaotic urge to taunt her creeps to my lips. "Sorry, babe—I don't exactly keep a dossier on my kills, and you clearly weren't worth remembering."

"Bet you'd remember me if we were back on that stage, with the Devil inside me. Bet you'd remember if I threw his words back at you." Her echoing, ethereal voice drops to something colder, sharper. "'The moment I learned of your plan, I knew I had to see it come to fruition with my own eyes. Well, the eyes of a rock idol, anyway.'"

Rock idol.

Rock idol.

The memory strikes me like a slap. One of those nights last year when I was on the run, hiding in a dingy motel in Barstow or Fresno or wherever the fuck it was. Only a few channels worked on that piece of shit television set—prime time garbage, corporate snooze fests, and good old MTV.

I remember her from her debut music video, that spine-tingling interview she gave on TRL with Carson Daly.

I marveled at her strong, muscular form that defied every provincial norm of what women should look like —especially now. How she pushed every boundary, questioned and defied the beast of the entertainment industry, and dared to write her own rules. How she exuded power, anarchy, and destruction. How she could flip from rapid-fire lyrical prowess to snarling, gravelly fury in an instant.

Despite her rebellion, it appeared the demons of Hollywood had gotten to her, given her a platform for her voice.

And so, she gave a voice to the unheard.

Or, at least, she tried.

That was before she met her untimely demise when the Devil possessed her body at a Halloween rock concert in a cemetery—*my* concert. *My* reaping.

"Summer Jones." Her name spills from my lips.

Her ghostly silhouette writhes above me, a glowing mist clinging to her like the ashes of my inferno. Her ghostly form still bears the appearance of her body right before she died—singed skin, exposed muscle and bone, hair midnight black and charred. "You let me burn," she growls, just like in one of her songs. "You caused the flames. You killed me."

In her moment of revelation, I finally unleash a surge of necromantic power through every pore, the raw energy slamming into her like a freight train and hurling her across the platform. I surge to my feet and blast another wave at the horde of spirits—dark magic rippling outward like a shock wave. Finally, they all scatter behind the 13 arches, like cockroaches fleeing from light.

But Summer doesn't run.

She rises from the obsidian stone with predatory grace, an ethereal punk rock goddess wreathed in spectral chains rattling like war drums. Her mouth hangs open in a silent scream, eyes blazing white-hot with supernatural fury. Power radiates from her translucent form in waves, death magic that matches my own, yet twisted by Hell's influence into something even more dangerous.

Two apex predators circling each other. A match made in Hellfire.

"Your body was already dying the moment Luci chose you as his mouthpiece." I examine my nails with mastered indifference and then flash her a sadistic grin. "Mortals weren't built for that kind of power. Brain, organs, everything just…shuts down. You were dead before the flames even touched you. The fire was just a cleanup anyway. You should have seen the Pit."

Summer doesn't find it amusing. Her ethereal form turns a deep shade of red, and I find myself backing up, knocking right into Mayhem's chest.

"Easy there, kitten," Mayhem purrs into my ear, hands gripping my arms protectively. "That mouth of yours is gonna be the end of you. Back off and let me rattle what's left of her."

"I'm a necromancer. Taking care of pains in my ass

like this one is my specialty," I mutter, trying to shrug out of his grip, but he only chuckles and pulls me closer, the cheeky fuck.

"I wouldn't piss her off if I were you. Violence and Vengeance are always looking for souls like hers—hungry and ready to serve. Push her too far, and one of them will snatch her right up. Then, she'll be a *real* pain in your ass."

I hate that he's right, hate the little caveat that not all souls stay unclaimed forever. The moment they give an inkling of their vice, one of the Primes will claim them. Eat them, torture them, demonify them—whatever floats their power-hungry boats. Still, despite his warning and offer, I grab his wrists and channel my fire magic to burn his skin. He lingers despite the pain, letting out one of those horribly timed moans before stumbling out of my way with a booming laugh. The fucking nerve of this guy.

Stalking toward the enraged spirit, hands crackling with magic, I murmur an ancient Hellspeak incantation under my breath, willing her ethereal form to bend to my will, to submit to my power.

But something stops me dead in my tracks.

The high-pitched, mournful screams of the surrounding spirits. They clutch their heads, writhing in agony, contorting in ways no human body ever could. Their translucent forms flicker like dying flames, barely clinging to what little power they have left. Some hurl themselves off the platform, back into the Pit they crawled out of. Others vanish entirely. Even Summer clutches her head, though she's still too powerful—too resilient. I spin around the platform, searching for the source of their torment, and my eyes narrow when I find it.

Find *him.*

Mayhem stands behind me, lightning crackling around his feet on the ancient stone. There's a feral, euphoric expression plastered across his features as he feeds on the pure mania radiating from the spirits. His long, spindly fingers twist and writhe in ways that make my stomach turn as he draws their essence into himself, forked tongue lolling from his mouth as he savors every drop.

"What are you doing?" I shout over their screams.

"Eating." His voice drops to something inhuman, like a recording played at half speed. "It's been forever since I've had a proper meal."

"You're devouring their sanity? They're fucking *ghosts*—"

"Don't care." His tongue flicks across those monstrous teeth. "They're delicious. You handle the rock star. I've got dinner to finish."

One by one, Mayhem devours the spirits. Some fall victim to his mania-feeding powers, others flee entirely, and a few have the fortitude to remain anchored to the platform. But I don't have time for any of them.

I only have eyes for Summer Jones.

"It's a shame you want to kill me." I tilt my head, flashing her a sardonic smile. "We could have been great friends."

"I don't want to be your friend." She takes her shackles in hand, spinning them like a lasso on her right side. "I want you to suffer."

"What a coincidence—I already am. So let's kiss and make up."

The sharp clang of her chains cracks through the air as lightning splits the sky above us. The links lash out, aiming for my wrists, legs, anything they can grab. She's an absolute marvel in her ghostly fury, fueled by anguish, caught between life and death but nowhere near powerful enough to bring me down.

After all, I'm a necromancer. I still hold all the cards.

Dodging her chains, I raise barriers of pure death magic, siphoning what few souls remain on the platform—the ones Mayhem hasn't devoured yet. Their forms streak toward my waiting hands from every curve of the platform. I stir the energy in circular motions, collecting souls by the handful like gathering smoke then hurling them in Summer's direction. Their essence feeds my power, creating walls of writhing ghosts to shield me from her assault.

Summer's voice comes as a muffled growl beyond the barrier of magic. "Wasn't enough to fuck us over in life, so now you're pulling the same shit in death too? You're pathetic."

"We have very different definitions of 'pathetic,' babe."

When her frustrated groan echoes throughout the expanse, I begin my incantation from before.

"By the monumental souls I have reaped,

I command this spirit whose form I seek,

Chain her essence, bind her might,

Make her mine with no will to fight."

Beyond my spectral wall of dead souls, I hear Summer's chains rattle to life. I watch through translucent, ghostly forms as she falls to her knees, and I will her shackles to bind her to the ground. She writhes against their hold, but my magic overpowers her— barely.

Fuck me, fresh souls sure are feisty. Makes sense, I suppose. They've got nothing left to lose—they just lost everything. But there's something about this one, something I can't quite pin down.

She's too strong. Too resilient. There's more to her than just another human body who got possessed by the Devil and shipped straight to Hell.

Perhaps He saw something in her. Perhaps none of this was an accident.

But the thought is ripped away when her voice cuts through the chaos in my head.

Her glowing white eyes illuminate sharp cheekbones, stark against ink-black hair that writhes around her face like it's underwater. Those eyes lock on mine, and spectral tears stream down her cheeks as she snarls through gritted teeth, "I'm going to be your worst fucking nightmare, October Winters. Every time you close your eyes, every time you think you've won—think a-fucking-gain. You'll never escape what you did to me."

The words should terrify me, but that's all they are—empty threats from a spectral pain in my ass who'll never get the chance to see me again. Not here, not anywhere.

Where do dead people go once their souls are banished in Hell? We're about to find the fuck out.

But before I get the chance, a blinding light burns through my retinas.

I throw up my leather sleeve to shield my face, the brightness searing even through closed eyelids. When I finally force my eyes open, watering and stinging, I find the source. In the middle-left quadrant, one of the arches tears itself apart with light. Insects pour out in a writhing, clicking mass: beetles with razor mandibles, spiders thick as my fist, centipedes that move like liquid nightmares. The air fills with the wet sound of chittering and the musty stench of decay.

Two hands punch through the swarm, emerging from the portal's maw. One is clawed flesh, hanging in strips from yellowed bone, fingernails black with rot.

The other is pure skeleton, joints snapping as the bones flex and grasp at the air.

That's when the cold dread seeps in, merciless as a winter storm burying everything in its path.

Despite my magical hold on her, Summer's body begins to move. Her protesting groan echoes throughout the platform as the spectral chains binding her lurch toward the portal. She fights against them, her ghostly form bucking as guttural screams tear from her throat. The chains tighten around her exposed ribs, yanking her backward, but, still, the fucking bitch persists. Finally, the chain around her neck snaps taut and drags her into the portal, her screams cutting off as she vanishes.

Just like that, Summer Jones's soul is claimed by a Prime.

The platform falls silent. The dead have retreated into the Pit. The bugs swarming the arch cease their languid crawling and take flight. I squint to read the inscription etched into the arch.

Fuck me.

Fuck. Me.

Mayhem's by my side suddenly, keeling over with sharp, unhinged laughter. "I fucking love when the universe has a sense of humor." His words grind against my nerves. "Oh, this is gonna be *fucking fabulous.* Your little pain in the ass just got sucked into the exact realm we're heading to."

I turn to face the demon, glaring daggers with a clenched jaw. "*You're* a pain in my ass."

"Baby, I would love to be."

I shove him forward, causing him to stumble over the satanic ram's maw carved into the platform's center. "Open the gate."

He flashes me that maddening grin. "Say please."

"Fuck you," I snarl. "Open the damn gate."

"Alright, alright. You don't have to be so hostile." His kaleidoscope eye flutters, painfully reminiscent of my own eye rolls, and he finally brings his palm to the left side of his face, where those monstrous teeth split his jaw in half. He bites into his own flesh, teeth squelching through skin as black, demonic ichor streams down his wrist and forearm like liquid night.

His hand hovers over the ram's gaping jaw, squeezing tight as his blood drips down its stone throat. "*Nightmares and Fear*," he whispers in perfect Hellspeak.

Within seconds, his demonic blood flows down the carved canal. The entire platform shudders as it rotates counterclockwise, grinding to a halt when it aligns perfectly with gate number Nine.

A voice echoes from the portal, ancient and terrible: "*Welcome, Mayhem, First of Chaos.*"

"Thanks for that," I grit through clenched teeth, quickly conjuring a fresh set of black boots on my feet with a wave of my hand. "I'd say this was fun, but as much as I love lying, I wouldn't want to give you false hope. Toodles."

"Hold your horses, baby girl." He grabs my elbow, yanking me backward before I can step toward the portal.

"What?" I spin around to face him, irritation flashing across my features.

"You're forgetting something. You need me."

"I need you like I need an asshole on my elbow, Mayhem," I snap, crossing my arms over my chest.

"You know, I was actually excited when Chaos gave me this job. I've been dying to meet you for centuries. The famous October Winters."

"Yeah, well, the famous October Winters has never needed a bodyguard before. I've always been fine on my own."

"Consider it a compliment, kitten. You're so high up the food chain now, you need protection," he purrs, stepping closer.

My voice hardens. "The last person who tried to protect me regretted it."

"Let me make that decision myself." He extends his hand, those spindly fingers wiggling like pale worms. "Take my hand."

"Gross, no."

"You can't get in without me. Opening the gate was just step one—it's the rules of permission. You'll get blasted back out the second you try to cross alone. Wanna test it?"

Fuck this place, and fuck its rules.

With an exasperated sigh, I begrudgingly take Mayhem's hand. His skin prickles against mine, soft electric currents rippling in waves and sending goose-bumps up my arms. It's a welcome sensation—a reminder I'm still alive, that my body is still solid, that I'm not some translucent, wandering jackass like the lost souls we just sent back to the Pit.

I don't know what lies beyond this portal, no idea what nightmares await me or what terrors will drag me into a grave a thousand years overdue.

All I know is there's a two-headed Prime who despises me and a vengeful spirit Hell-bent on revenge who just got consumed by that very same Prime. As far as I'm concerned, I'm walking straight into the suicide mission of a lifetime.

I fucking hate dead people.

Especially the ones who refuse to stay that way.

YOU WILL GROW OLD HERE, OCTOBER WINTERS.
TRACK FIVE
TAKE A LOOK AROUND
YOUR SKIN WILL SHRIVEL AND FRAY, YOUR BONES WILL TURN TO DUST.
YOU'LL BECOME A THOUSAND-YEAR-OLD PILE OF NOTHING.

TRACK FIVE
TAKE A LOOK AROUND

If the Chaos Realm was a psychedelic fever dream, the Nightmare and Fear Realm is like waking up in a sealed grave six feet under.

Darkness swallows me the second I step through the portal. The oppressive heat from the Ring of the Thirteen vanishes replaced by biting cold, the kind that's so brutal, it tricks your body. Your fingers feel warm even as frostbite sets in, your mind's convinced it's heating up while you're actually freezing to death.

That's what this feels like. Death.

Nothingness. Loneliness.

So all-consuming, it forms a pit in my stomach and threatens to turn me inside out.

My fingers instinctively rub together, and I breathe a sigh of relief, feeling the soft pads of my thumb and index finger. Thank fuck, I can still feel. They trail up my leather jacket—good, it's still there. I take a deep breath and inhale the sharp, unmistakable musk of death and decay. A questionable choice, but at least I'm still breathing.

I'm not dead. Not yet.

Then why can't I fucking see?

The silence suffocates me as I force my feet forward, but it's quickly shattered when my boot collides with something squishy and wet. A shiver races up my spine, spreading across every nerve until it pools in my stomach and curdles into pure unease. Before I can snap my fingers to conjure a flame, a sickeningly shrill whisper brushes against my ear.

"You're going to die down here."

The voice isn't one I recognize. It's nothing like Mayhem's mismatched cadence or the Devil's warm promise. This is something else entirely—haunting, disembodied. It feels inches from my face, yet I sense no other presence. No breathing, no warmth, nothing. Just this eerie whisper, promising my death.

"You'll be trapped forever, caged like the rabid dog you are. You will starve, desperate for power just out of reach. You will rot in Hell, October Winters, and we will all celebrate your demise."

My heart leaps into my throat the second a pair of long, thin fingers find my waist. Instinctively, I ignite a fistful of fire and whirl around to face whatever fool is bold enough to touch me.

I'm met with Mayhem's shiny, monstrous grin.

He's terrifying in the darkness, my Hellfire casting shadows across the exposed muscle stretched taut over his cheekbones before they disappear into his gums. The light reflects in his void-like eye and illuminates his kaleidoscopic one. My flames splinter through them like light in a prism, throwing shards of color across my skin in patterns that shift every time he breathes. For a moment, I'm helpless. Frozen. Unable to look away.

"Voices getting to you, beautiful?" he murmurs, his voice nothing like that whisper.

"Voices?" I ask, breaking free from my trance.

"You'll learn to tune them out. Pesky little fucks." Mayhem reaches for the flame in my hand, splitting it and claiming a piece for himself. He walks toward what I assume is a wall, though it looks nothing like one. He holds his flame against the surface, revealing a pitch-black panel stretched with what appears to be leather.

From underneath, skeletal hands and screaming faces push against the material, as if bodies are trapped behind the wall itself.

I've seen some creepy shit in my life. Hell, horror movies are practically my Friday night comedy fix. Don't get me started on Pestilence Underlings. Even my demonic escort's appearance makes me squirm. But this wall of writhing limbs and eyeless faces takes the fucking cake for creepiest thing I've ever witnessed.

Instinctively, I step closer.

The faces crumple in agony, gaping mouths slack in perpetual screams. The hands reach for me, fingers curling desperately, trying to drag me into the void with them. "What *is* this?"

"Souls claimed by the twins. Pretty sure Joan Jett's stuck in there now."

"Joan Jett's still alive." I shoot him a confused look. But when he wiggles his eyebrows, I get it. "Summer Jones, dipshit. Her name is Summer Jones."

"Same difference."

I pull my leather jacket tighter with my free hand, turning away from the wall. That's when the eerie voice speaks again. "You will grow old here, October Winters. Your skin will shrivel and fray, your bones will turn to dust. You'll become a thousand-year-old pile of nothing."

"Shut the fuck up," I mutter under my breath. I glance at Mayhem. "What *is* that voice?"

"Fear Underlings. They're stuck in the walls too. They whisper your greatest fears to drive you insane. But not as insane as I can make you, promise."

Wonderful. My greatest fears are death and growing old. I'm no better than a fucking human. "What do they whisper to you?"

"Nothing. They love me down here." His unsettling grin returns, making my insides churn. "Plus, I don't fear anything. I'm batshit."

"Lucky me," I mutter. "So where are we exactly? Is there a light switch anywhere?"

"'Fraid not. If anyone's lucky here, it's me—having a fire witch by my side beats trying to navigate the labyrinth with one good eye."

"One *good* eye?"

"The black one doesn't see shit down here. The other one sees everything, but multiplied by, like, six. And with extra colors. Trippy as fuck."

"And you said we're in a labyrinth?"

"Oh yeah. Massive fucking maze where billions of Underlings whisper your worst fears on repeat, all while you're stepping on bugs." He points his flame toward the ground, and I finally see it.

Every insect imaginable carpets the entire maze. Spiders. Ants. Roaches. Centipedes. The fucking works.

"Jesus fucking Christ, I hate it down here." I step back instinctively, my boot crunching on something that was definitely alive once.

"Y'know, for someone as old as you, I'm surprised you've never once come down for a little visit." His tone carries that familiar mocking edge. "Think you're too good for the likes of us?"

"If you'd put half the souls down here, would you want to visit?" I snap, gesturing around the darkness.

"Or did you conveniently forget what we just went through back at the Ring?"

"What, that? That was just the welcoming committee. You're gonna get the whole party up in here." His grin widens, showing too many teeth.

"Fabulous," I groan, conjuring two more flames in my palms before whispering "float." I watch them rise above my head, casting flickering light across the nightmarish expanse. "C'mon. I need to get to the twins."

"Slow your roll, kitten." He places an arm on the wall behind me, caging me in from one side, and I instinctively press my back against it despite the grooves of the souls writhing beneath.

"Don't call me kitten."

"Why not?" He chuckles, patronizing yet annoyingly sexy. "You're like a little black void—all claws and attitude. It's fucking adorable."

I grit my teeth. "You know what's adorable? Orange cats. Dumb as rocks, zero survival instinct. Remind you of anyone?"

"Ouch." He doesn't budge when I shove against his chest, simply arching one hairless brow, the exposed muscle contracting with the movement. His forked tongue flicks across the right side of his mouth, where human lips curl into a predatory grin. "You trying to get away from me?"

"Trying to get you off me."

"If *this* is how you're trying to get me off, I have

notes." He leans in closer, breathing me in, that eerie kaleidoscope eye focused entirely on me. "You can't just waltz into this realm like you own the fuckin' place. Because you don't. They *hate* you here. The minute they get a whiff of you, they'll be picking at you like meat off a bone. But…" He leans in even closer, his voice dropping to a purr so electric, it feels like static from a radio. "If you want to mask your scent…I have a few ideas."

My eyes flutter shut despite my better judgment. The heat rolling off his body is chaotic—unstable—and it sends an electric rush straight through me.

"Would you rather be Demon-Kissed or kissed by a demon? Choice is yours. I'll enjoy it either way." His voice is like a caress against my skin, and frustration boils within me as my body betrays my mind.

My eyes narrow in contempt, but something hungry stirs underneath, the need to toy with him the way he's toying with me. Demon-Kissing doesn't work on a witch like me—it never does. The ability to feed off human vices requires something I stopped being a long time ago. Enough Debauchery demons have tried and failed over the years, but Mayhem doesn't need to know that.

His face is so close, I can feel the electric currents radiating off his skin. I let my features relax into a small, predatory smirk, eyelids hooding as my fingers find the collar of his mesh shirt. I trace the ever-moving ichor scars carved into his skin, trailing up to his throat.

That kaleidoscope eye spins faster as I dig my thumb into the hollow where his neck meets his jaw, wrap my fingers around his neck, and pull him closer.

"We both have jobs to do," I say, voice cold as steel. "I can't afford to let you distract me."

The chuckle that rumbles from his chest is warm as honey, traveling up my spine and melting every frigid nerve. "Baby, I think a distraction is *exactly* what the Devil ordered."

I release him with an eye roll and push away. "Ew."

We begin trudging through the endless chasms littered with insects, and, with every step, something scurries up my leg or crunches under my boots. I don't give them a second thought—they're clearly the standard décor, playing on humanity's primal fear of creepy crawlies.

My familiar should feel right at home.

My thoughts drift to the dormant creature around my finger—the obsidian ring that will inevitably need awakening for the wicked work ahead. I expected to hear Lovejoy's voice by now, but he's been eerily silent since…well, everything.

But that's the beauty of turning him into jewelry.

Jewels can't talk back.

Necromancy is a dark, sacred art, one that can easily overwhelm a common witch. It's an art I've mastered, twisting every rule to suit my needs, from manipulating souls to raising the dead.

But I've never placed a Divine soul in a sentient creature before.

Plus, the angelic Nephilim, much like myself, operate above magical law, breaking rules that bind everyone else. I learned that shit the hard way.

Fucking Angels.

"You want to know what I think?" my demonic escort's voice cuts through my thoughts.

I feel another eye roll coming on but evade it by clenching my jaw instead. "No, but I'm sure you're going to tell me anyway."

"I think you need someone to put you in your place."

"I know where my place is." Another bug squelches beneath my sole. "It's above you, your Prime, and all your moronic uncles."

"Above me, under me, on your side next to me…I'm not picky."

I ignore the quip by kicking away another swarm of bugs. "Can you make yourself useful and clear a path here? Swear to the Devil, I'm going to find roaches in my panties for the next decade."

"Never thought I'd envy a roach, but here we are," Mayhem mutters beneath his breath, and this time, the eye roll wins.

Mayhem shoots a blast of magic at the swarm at our feet. The insects erupt in gut-wrenching squeals, scattering in panic. Some writhe and twitch on the ground while others simply drop dead, flipped on their backs.

He crouches, running those too-long fingers through the soot covering the ground. With a wave of his hand, he beckons me closer.

"C'mere. Look." He begins drawing circles in the soot. Two large ones and then a smaller one interconnecting them. "This realm isn't like the others. It's got wings." He points to the left circle. "This one's the Fear Wing. All the Underlings live here—ghouls, banshees, wraiths, you name it." He taps the right circle. "This is the Nightmare Wing. You don't wanna go here. Anyone who goes in doesn't come back, and if, by some odd chance, they do, well—they might as well stay there."

"What's the deal with it?"

"It's the central hub for Nightmare Feedings. It's how the twins feed off humans from their own realm. It's all connected—like dial-up."

"So it's like a demonic kitchen or something?" I try to make sense of the logistics.

"More like a refrigerator. Every nightmare from every human is stored there, and sometimes, the nightmares come to life."

"Fascinating."

For a moment, I wonder how many of Lovejoy's nightmares are in there. 80 years Marked means countless feedings.

And somewhere, deep in that demonic refrigerator,

is the nightmare they pulled from me, the memory of the day my life changed forever.

I'll never forgive them for that.

Mayhem finally points to the smallest circle. "This right here is the Apex, where the Prime lives. Their throne room, if you will. This is where we need to go."

"How do we get there?"

"Through the maze. Don't worry, I know this place like the back of my hand." He shows me the back of his hand; the dark, raised scars start to animate, forming their own labyrinthine pattern.

He rises, towering over me by a full foot. I crane my neck to study him, taking in every dark hollow of his features, every monstrous detail that should send me running.

Normally, I don't give a damn about demons or their sob stories. But this one…this one is different. I saw it when he devoured those spirits. There's something wild and unpredictable about him that goes beyond typical chaos. You can't blame a girl for her curiosity.

Or a cat, for that matter.

The question escapes before I can stop it. "What's your story, Mayhem?"

"Oh, it's a real page-turner. New York Times Bestseller for five centuries in a row. I'm arguably as old as you and three times more unhinged. Born in chaos, raised by chaos, became chaos incarnate. Spoiler alert: everyone dies, including my victims' therapists." His grin widens impossibly. "They're my favorites, you know—therapists. They know everyone's secrets, and I eat secrets for breakfast." He runs a hand through his dark, near-black hair.

My scrutinizing gaze doesn't falter as he continues walking, leading me deeper into the labyrinth. "And how exactly does someone like you become a First of Chaos?"

"Hard work meets opportunity. Secret to life. Best breakfast I've ever had."

His words make absolutely zero sense, and I have no patience to decode the ramblings of a mentally unstable demon.

A sudden groan catches us both off guard, a low, guttural sound reminiscent of the damned noises my minions make when I raise them from the dead. I check over my shoulder, searching the walls—but there's no source.

Then, we fall into that deadly-quiet stillness, the kind every horror film ever made taught me precedes a jump scare.

THUNK.

My body slams into the floor, face and hands colliding with the cold, writhing insects. The urge to retch takes over as I spit out the crushed remains between my lips. An unyielding weight pins me from above as I attempt to rise to my feet.

I'm flipped over, straddled by an ethereal corpse

animated by demonic magic. Decrepit, skeletal fingers wrap around my throat, cutting off the circulation at my jugular. I gasp, and the nauseating stench of death and decay floods my lungs, making me choke. The white-haired creature shrieks in my face, her glowing eyes streaming spectral tears down hollow cheeks.

Great. A motherfucking banshee.

"Get the fuck off me," I choke out, struggling beneath its grasp. Beside me, three more creatures circle Mayhem, salivating at the sight of him while he practically drools over them in return. Banshees are Fear Underlings, harbingers of death who sense the end before it strikes—the ultimate secret.

And Mayhem is eyeing them like they're a stack of buttermilk pancakes.

The Chaos Underling strikes with lightning-quick, viperine swiftness. He clutches the throats of two banshees simultaneously, cutting off their spectral circulation as their bone-chilling wails die in their throats. I watch with horrified fascination as he literally inhales their screams, drawing their death-song into himself like a vacuum.

Their bodies go limp in his grasp, tattered burial dresses and white hair somehow more lifeless than they were even in death. He discards them like garbage, lunging toward me to seize the creature choking me. Grabbing it by the shoulder, he sinks his claws deep into its decrepit, pale flesh, and blessed air floods back into my lungs.

"Don't touch my fucking kitten." His voice drops to a demonic growl that reverberates through the entire chasm before he swallows the Fear Underling whole.

Actually whole.

His jaw unhinges just like it did back at the Ring, dropping nearly to the ground as he devours the banshee in one horrifying gulp. Its death-wail cuts off abruptly in his throat as his jaw closes. He licks his razor-sharp teeth, flashing me that deranged grin. In this Hellish light, he's a creature of immeasurable hunger, of insatiable appetite. He is exactly as he claimed—born of chaos, raised by chaos, chaos incarnate.

He stalks toward me, that swagger in his step far too confident, too satisfied. He towers over me, and the way he runs his tongue across those freakish lips tells me he's considering devouring me next.

Instead, he extends his long, spindly fingers toward me.

I catch my breath, transfixed by his hand. The geometric scars carved into his flesh shift in slow, hypnotic waves, twisting and curling like a cat stretching in sunlight. His fingers are impossibly long and skeletal—pure uncanny valley. They shouldn't exist in these proportions, yet you wouldn't notice until they're right in front of you, demanding attention.

Nothing about his anatomy makes sense. His scars. His hands. His mouth.

Yet everything in my twisted mind finds him irresistible to explore.

Before he can pull me to my feet, another pack of decrepit corpses—wraiths, I realize—comes crawling around the corner.

Motherfuckers.

Leaping to my feet, I reach into my back pocket and pull a cigarette from my trusty pack. With a snap of my fingers, a flame catches paper, and I'm eager to calm the frustration churning in my gut.

"Really?" Mayhem says. "Lighting up at a time like this?"

Wonderful. Another person—if you can call him a person—to berate me for my smoking. I hurl a ball of fire at a screeching corpse crawling on all fours toward me and take another drag.

"Save the lecture. I'm a thousand years old—I don't give a fuck what goes in my body."

Four more wraiths swirl toward us, hands outstretched like claws. I lift an arm to shield myself, but Mayhem's already moving. He steps in front of me, unleashing a whirl of chaos magic that blasts them into the wall—straight into the gaping mouths of the creatures living inside it. They devour the spirits in seconds.

Before I can lower my arm, Mayhem turns and hauls me upright. He plucks the cigarette from between my lips and takes a drag so long, the ember nearly reaches the filter. Smoke curls from the gaps in his monstrous teeth, seeping from his nostrils as he grins. With deliberate slowness, he flicks the spent butt to the floor, where it vanishes into the writhing carpet of insects.

He leans in so close that when he exhales, it's directly into my mouth—slow, deliberate, making me take what was mine to begin with.

"There's only one thing you should give a fuck about putting inside you." His eyes don't leave mine. "And that would be me."

His words sink into me like poison, setting every nerve ending ablaze. I can't fathom what Chaos demons truly feel. From my experience, they don't read minds—they devour them. The thought is dangerously tempting: allowing a demon to consume my consciousness, obliterate my memories, erase my pain.

Fuck me, it's *terrifyingly* tempting.

Instead, I deflect his advance. Again.

"For the love of all that is unholy, you're insufferable."

That laugh—maniacal, sinister, and far too satisfied—echoes through the labyrinth. "I know." His grin sharpens. "And I just *love* making you squirm."

His serpentine tail flicks, slow and deliberate, coiling as if it's dying to touch me, and I know damn well where his head is at.

I refuse to let his blatant flirtation distract me any

further, to let him think he's the one in control here. He's anything but. Just because his filter is less corroded than mine doesn't mean I'm the submissive in this dynamic.

"What makes you delusional enough to think I'd fuck you?" I hold up a hand before he can respond. "Wait—better question: in what twisted universe would I *actually* fuck you?"

"This one." He closes the distance between us. His voice drops low, gravelly like static through a radio. "Word gets around, y'know? And fucking demons isn't exactly a new concept for you. You said so yourself."

Loudmouth sons of bitches. Should've known one of Cherry's Underlings would blab—fucking the Devil's Second is Pulitzer-worthy gossip down here. I scoff and wave my hand dismissively. "Debauchery demons don't count. They're transactional."

His fingers graze my waist before I see them— spindly digits tracing the threads of my jeans from my hip upward. "See, that's the problem. They fucked you because they *had* to. I *want* to fuck you because I can't stop thinking about the sounds you'll make when you come for me."

The labyrinth suddenly feels suffocating—walls closing in, those rotting hands reaching from the panels like they're seconds from dragging me under. But the walls stay still. The hands don't move. Only the space between us shrinks.

His fingers trail up my side and find my arm. The

sensation is electric—sharp little jolts that should repel me. Instead, I lean into the pain, into the needling static against my skin. It makes me feel something other than anger, something miles away from the anguish that's been eating me alive.

It would be so easy. Balance on my toes, pull him down, kiss him until neither of us can think straight. Not that he ever thinks straight to begin with.

Except that monstrous mouth—all those teeth, that forked tongue—would make it one Hell of a messy exchange.

The gulp in my throat is pathetic. The dryness is worse. "Listen, weirdo. This whole flirting thing is cute. Entertaining, even. But don't get any ideas. If you think I'm getting anywhere near *that*," I gesture at his body, "then you're crazier than I thought."

He flashes me a sharp-toothed grin. "I'm a Chaos demon, baby."

"Exactly. A *demon*. And if anything were to ever happen between us, it's going to be on my terms. No demon form."

"What?" he snaps. "But my joints bend in the coolest fucking ways. That's half the fun. I'm more flexible than you are. Probably. Let's find out—" His hands find my waist again, and I jolt backward.

"Nope. Not happening. If you're going to fuck me, you're wearing a glamour."

It's his turn to jolt back. His expression is a mess of

incredulous smiles and feigned offense. "A *glamour*? That's the demonic equivalent of wrapping it up. This is tragic. I might as well take a vow of celibacy."

"I'm sure you can find someone else who appreciates the full chaotic package. But if you want me? Those are my terms. Glamour only."

"Fucking meat sacks," he mutters under his breath as I begin trudging through the rest of the labyrinth. His footsteps pick up behind me. "Why not start with human form and *then* work our way up?"

"I'm done with this conversation, Mayhem."

In a flash, Mayhem teleports in front of me so I slam into his body. His sadistic grin would be cute if it weren't so damn irritating. "So, what you're saying is…I have a chance."

I groan. "Do you *want* me to kill you?"

"Killing the First of Chaos will land you in deeper shit than the septic tank you're already drowning in with the twins. Do you really want to be on another Prime's list when you're on so many already?"

The fucker's got a point. Deflated, I sigh. "Whatever."

But that shit-eating grin burns into my brain. "Thought so."

I lose track of how long we've been in this damned labyrinth. Every turned corner, every dead end, drives me closer and closer to insanity—though I can't tell if that's the maze or just Mayhem's influence rubbing off on me. I've learned to silence the insidious whispers from the walls with practiced ease, allowing my mind to focus on the ice-cold dread pooling in my veins as I brace for attack around every corner. Fear Underlings—handfuls of wraiths, banshees, and poltergeists—sniff us out the deeper we get into the maze, threatening to tear us apart limb from limb for infiltrating their lair.

Mayhem, of course, is welcome. But I am not.

Still, it doesn't stop him from making a literal meal out of them.

"So…you given any thought to how you're gonna dig yourself out of this mess? What exactly did you do, anyway? I've heard bits and pieces, but I'm shit at separating fact from fiction. You know, voices and all that." He licks his fingers clean after devouring another wraith.

"Wouldn't you like to know."

"I would. Because if you have any secret plans to set this insect orgy on fire and peace the fuck out, I'd like to get my hazmat suit ready." I don't dignify his words with a response and take the next left at the fork in the maze. He continues. "Though, on second thought, if you *do* have some secrets up your sleeve, I'm all for it. Element of surprise. Catch the fuckers off guard. Might be better if I don't know. More authentic that way."

I allow the demon to ramble on, with his thoughts pivoting and making mental U-turns on a dime, when a brilliant thought comes to mind. *Insect orgy on fire.* The fucker might have a point. I conjure another flame in my hand, illuminating the corridor before us. The insects furl inward and retreat further into the walls by my blinding light.

But, as always, my brilliant impulses create a bigger fucking mess.

Another pack of Underlings rounds the corner, salivating at the sight of me. They completely ignore Mayhem, fixated on the flames dancing in my palms as I prepare to incinerate them. Wraiths circle overhead like vultures, banshees unleash their bone-chilling death-wails, and ghouls claw their way up from the ground, insects streaming across their putrid flesh.

Rotting skin and exposed bone, decayed sinew and weeping muscle, tattered burial shrouds and soul-piercing screams—Fear Underlings are every human's worst nightmare.

But they aren't mine. They just get on my fucking nerves.

I brace for impact as they surge toward me. The voices in the walls return, shattering the mental barrier I'd constructed. They crescendo now, layering over each other in a cacophony of psychological warfare on endless repeat.

"You're going to die here."

I can still hear the words even when they've moved on to other torments. Layer upon layer, they hurl every fear they think haunts my sleepless nights.

But then, they speak the words that shatter my composure completely.

"He will replace you with your daughter."

And all my flames disintegrate.

The Underlings' glowing, predatory eyes illuminate the corridor in a sickly light. Snarling, clicking, wet-popping sounds fill my ears as they surge closer, ready to tear me apart. But the walls keep taunting.

"She will replace you as the Devil's Second."

The rage erupts from my chest along with a different form of magic entirely. It isn't the searing heat of my flames, but the dark, siphoning, soul-sucking torque of my death magic.

I consume them all, one by one. The Underlings, the voices, even the insects crawling beneath my feet.

Their demonic essence flows into my waiting palms, tears streaming down my face as the sheer power envelops me like a drug.

The rush is intoxicating.

Hundreds of demonic souls extinguished in seconds, plunging us into absolute darkness. I've never felt more alive than I do surrounded by death and devastation.

Silence returns, broken only by my ragged breathing and the sound of my racing heart.

When Mayhem's hand finds my shoulder, every nerve in my body stills.

"You're fucking magnificent."

I conjure another flame above us. His head is tilted

back, shoulders rolling as he fights the arousal off him in pulses.

I can feel it. We both can. The rush. The need. The hunger.

And after that exhilarating massacre, I'd fuck him right here on this insect-littered ground, demon form and all.

That's when my eyes drop to the floor. At my feet lie hundreds of black soul orbs.

"Shit," I mutter.

"What's wrong?" Mayhem groans, his voice thick with desire.

I gesture at the demonic souls scattered around us. "Dead Underlings."

"And?"

Lucifer's voice echoes in my head: *"You are not, under any circumstances, permitted to harm any of the demons whilst inside their realms."* Yet, here they lie, deader than dead. The Devil will have my head before Nightmares and Fear even get the chance.

I look down at the ring on my finger. With gritted teeth, I reluctantly remove it and place it in my palm. Mayhem watches me with growing confusion, his kaleidoscope eye spinning frantically.

His voice drops to a shaky whisper. "What are you doing?"

"Mitigating risks." I hover my hand above my palm,

fingers moving in slow, deliberate circles as I prepare to cast the spell.

I didn't want to do this.

Not here. Not in front of Mayhem. Not in the one realm where I'm most vulnerable.

But desperate times call for desperate fucking measures, and I need to cover my ass.

"Lovejoy, awaken."

YOUR EYE IS DOING THAT THING AGAIN.
WHAT THING?
TRACK SIX
COMFORTABLE LIAR
THE ONE WHERE...IT STARES...AND I.. CAN'T...
CAN'T WHAT, OCTOBER?
...LOOK AWAY.

TRACK SIX

COMFORTABLE LIAR

My black ring springs to life, its curled edges trembling and unfurling into a glorious, penny-sized scorpion. I wiggle my fingers again, whispering another incantation, and within seconds, he triples in size, growing to the length of my palm.

The creature remains statue-still, as scorpions do when they're deciding whether you're predator or prey. Then, he begins to move in rapid, stuttering advances across my palm, stopping when he realizes he has nowhere to go.

"Hi, handsome," I sneer at my familiar. "Have a nice nap?"

October. Declan Lovejoy's voice reverberates through my skull, laced with anguish. *What have you done to me?*

Hearing his voice again is both jarring and unexpected, sending a visceral reaction through me. My nerves are on fire, stinging my body as his words echo in my head against my will. Nero never spoke to me, no matter how badly I wished he could. The only voices I've ever heard are those of the dead. This is going to be one Hell of a learning curve.

"Oh, please. You know exactly what I did. Don't act like you can't see everything that's happened since I shoved your own blessed butter knife through your heart."

I place my scorpion on the ground, where he nearly vanishes among the sea of insects. They immediately scatter, creating a perfect circle of clear dirt for him to explore. Maybe they sense the remnants of his Divine soul trapped inside, or perhaps they recognize a witch's familiar in their midst. No, that's giving these fucking bugs too much credit. If all it took to clear them was my scorpion, I should have awakened him sooner.

But I already had one insufferable man by my side. I didn't need two.

I crouch, stepping into his clearing. My heart nearly stops as I take in my familiar—those eight delicate legs, two massive pincers, and that magnificent tail arched behind him. He's a beautiful specimen, his exoskeleton gleaming obsidian in the light of my twin flames illuminating the labyrinth. Devil knows I missed him more than I care to admit.

But the moment my finger reaches out to caress his

armored shell, the little creature backs away, stinger coiled and poised to strike.

It's amazing how quickly the bitter truth can stab you in the chest and twist the blade.

Where are we? Lovejoy asks, his words sending waves of rage crashing through me. I didn't expect such a primal reaction to his voice, but I should have known better. The wounds are still fresh, memories still razor-sharp.

The only saving grace is knowing he's mine to torment forever.

"The only place your soul would have gone if I hadn't gotten to it first." I flash him a predatory grin.

His claws twitch, opening and closing as reality sinks in. *Hell? Is this Hell?*

"The Nightmare and Fear Realm, to be precise." The sadistic edge to my voice sends delicious shivers up my spine. "You should be thanking me, really—an eternity serving me beats rotting in this cesspit."

I remember what he told me that night we were reunited. It was just days ago—how he'd been Marked by the Nightmares and Fear Primes, how they stole 80 years of sleep from him, how he'd been in agony every night, tormented by Nightmare Feedings, haunted by creatures that threatened to shred his sanity. In that moment, I pitied him, especially after experiencing Nightmare Feeding myself. I know firsthand how it feels to be mind-fucked, and I'd never let those bastards do it again.

Devil only knows what they would have done to his soul if they'd claimed it when I killed him. But the twins being trapped down here and my desperate need for a bargaining chip created the perfect storm.

Come to serve your sentence, then? my familiar practically spits in my mind. *I'd rather the Primes devour us both and put us out of our misery before I spend a second serving you.*

I roll my eyes. "How is it that you're even more dramatic as a scorpion than you ever were alive? Let's cut to the chase—I'm about to give you a crash course in Familiar 101. The syllabus is simple: you listen to every single thing I say and shut the fuck up about it. Got it?"

I'd rather claw my eyes out.

"So you could see even less than you already do? Lovejoy, I thought you were smarter than that." I pick my familiar up by the tail, sending small waves of magic through my fingers to anchor him. His little claws struggle against the hold, but my magic wins. "Here's how this works. You see those demonic soul orbs down there?" I nod toward the small pile. "Of course you don't—we already established that. I need you to absorb those little shits into your stinger and keep them there until we're topside. Understand?"

You're barking fucking mad if you think I'd do anything you ask.

"I'm afraid you don't have a choice, handsome. I own you. You do as I say, or I won't hesitate to make this much harder than it needs to be."

Over my dead body.

"Been there, done that." I drop him to the ground and shove him toward the pile. "Go on."

The little shit just stands there, defying me, grating on my nerves with every passing second. The longer we sit here with evidence of dead demons threatening to damn me, the faster my survival odds dwindle.

I tap into my familiar's mind, clawing for any part of him I can control. But he fucking resists, just like Summer resisted my necromancy. What the Hell is wrong with this goddamn place? It's like it was designed to weaken me, to humiliate me, to prove I'm not the witch I thought I was.

I'll fucking show them.

I wage war against Lovejoy's will, planting my feet shoulder-width apart in a battle stance. Sweat drips down my neck as my nails bite into my palms, teeth grinding so hard, my canines might crack. Try as I might, I can't fucking break him.

"C'mon, you little fucking bitch—*just take them*," I snarl as he fights against my power. The push and pull between my magic and his resistance is unlike anything I've ever experienced. It's like slamming into an invisible wall repeatedly, my knuckles white-hot and scream-ing. Finally, I suck in the soul of a nearby Hellspawn, using its life force to bulldoze past the barrier and over-power my familiar.

In seconds, a rush of heat floods through me—power, raw and unhinged, fills me and roars like an engine coming to life. Curling my fingers inward, I force Lovejoy to absorb the demonic soul orbs into his stinger. They vanish in an instant.

This new reality is Hell compared to what it was with Nero. With him, communication was seamless—just a thought, and he'd obey without question. No arguments. No attitude. No bullshit.

Dealing with Lovejoy is like raising a petulant child.

My familiar curls into a trembling ball at my feet, wrapping his tail around his body as he finally regains control of his limbs. Before he can skitter away, I pin him in place with my magic and crouch once more. My voice is a low, haunting growl.

"You wanted forever—congratulations, you fucking got it. The sooner you accept what I say and be a good little boy about it, the smoother the rest of eternity will be for both of us."

I'm suddenly painfully aware Mayhem witnessed this entire exchange. He leans against the maze wall, fingers absentmindedly toying with the limbs and digits as they jut from the stone, staring at me like I'm his next meal.

But there's something else in his mismatched gaze,

something that looks dangerously close to judgment. And I have zero tolerance for that shit.

"What?" I snap viciously, practically spitting the word at him.

"I've never been so turned on watching a woman degrade a bug before."

"*Arachnid.*" The correction claws its way out of my throat. I don't look at him, focusing instead on my familiar. "And you can save the perverted commentary for literally any other time. I'm two seconds away from lighting this whole place on fire. Get a fucking clue."

Moved on so quickly, have you? Lovejoy's voice slithers through my head again. *With a demon, no less? Your hypocrisy is astonishing.*

"Jealous much?" I saunter toward the scorpion, who skitters away from me, desperate to hide, to escape.

But he can't.

Something deep inside anchors him to me, and no matter how badly he wants to flee, our bond won't allow it.

I crouch to his level again, still towering over his pathetic form. He's so small, my Nero—not my Nero— so helpless. A sadistic smirk tugs at my lips as I pick him up by the stinger and dangle him in front of my face.

"Hate seeing me with someone else, don't you, Lovejoy?" I speak louder now, because I need Mayhem to hear this, need Lovejoy to know it's not a game, even if it is. "So many big emotions trapped in such a tiny body. Your brain's no bigger than a flea. And those poor little eyes, that blurry vision." I tilt my head, examining him like an insect pinned to a board. "It's a shame, really. Fucking him in front of you would be such a waste."

The delicious, *delicious* thrill of feeling his torment is like opening presents on Christmas morning. That first sip of Coke. The initial drop on a roller coaster. My body erupts in shivers of pleasure and satisfaction, knowing I pushed the right buttons, knowing I could *destroy* him with a simple threat.

Even an orgasm couldn't replace this feeling.

I want nothing more than to hurt him, to torment him the way he tormented me—make him feel every bit of betrayal, every ache of heartbreak. My wounds are still raw, and I can't shake the image of him driving his holy blade deep into my little Nero's scorpion's body.

Magic crackles at my curling fingertips, ready to inflict the kind of pain he deserves.

But all I see is Nero's body.

Not Lovejoy. Not the bastard who betrayed me. Just my familiar—my best friend trapped in this nightmare because I couldn't let either of them go.

The question burns: should I have let them both die? Is an eternity of this torture worth it?

My hand trembles. I can't do it, can't bear to watch Nero's form writhe in agony, even if it would hurt the soul inside him. Even if Lovejoy deserves every second of it.

I also can't let the doubt consume me. Not now. I've got a fucking job to do. As always.

I wave my hand toward the scorpion. Instead of inflicting pain, I simply transform him back into a ring and twist him onto my finger, right where he belongs.

Where I control this mess I've made.

"Wow." Mayhem's at my side again, making me jump. "You weren't kidding about the turning-me-into-earrings thing." His gaze flits to my ring. "He must be the one who broke your heart."

The slight tic in my jaw makes it obvious. "He played with fire and got burned."

"So you turned him into jewelry. *Fuck*, that's hot."

I turn to face him, confusion knitting my brows. "Hot?"

"Yeah. He fucked you over, so instead of just killing him, you turned him into your familiar, forcing him to do your bidding against his better judgment—against his damn will. And it gets better. You turn him into a piece of jewelry when you're done using him, and then you cuck him into watching you fuck the Devil? It's savage. Insane. And *exactly* what I would do."

His response, the way his chaotic body practically thrums with excitement and admiration, reminds me of a golden retriever on acid—tripping balls and salivating over its owner. The way his kaleidoscope eye spins, quickening and slowing with his level of excitement, is an enigma I don't pretend to understand. Demonic biology is complicated enough without factoring in the Chaos Broodline, but something about this Underling intrigues me, has me wondering if it's all a ruse, a perfectly orchestrated ploy to catch me off guard.

Demons don't love. They can't. It's not an ability they're born with. The only loyalty they have is to their Prime, and even that's a stretch. It's sire bonds and indentured servitude masked as devotion. Love might as well be rocket science to a demon: unnecessary.

But the way this demon looks at me, with those wild, unhinged eyes and that monstrous grin…

There's something more than chaos there.

"Hey." He pulls me from my thoughts. "You deserve better, you know. Luckily, I'm here now."

"You had one second of sincerity and immediately ruined it." I push ahead, boots squelching through the decay. "Have you ever tried not being a perverted asshole for five consecutive minutes?"

"My record is two and a half." That careless shrug, the smug tilt of his mouth—it shouldn't work on me. It really, really shouldn't. But clearly, my body is a mother-fucking traitor. "But for real, you walk on water and never ask anyone to consume your body and blood— though I'd happily do both if you'd let me."

I shoot him a cynical glare, one step away from

lighting his ass on fire again. "Are you going somewhere with this?"

"Sort of. I tend to start sentences and get distracted by other thoughts, especially when the hottest, most powerful woman in the Underworld is glaring daggers at me."

My hand smacks his chest as I playfully shove him aside.

"Alright, alright—serious mode. I can do this." He inhales sharply, shaking his limbs as if prepping for the longest run of his life. When he finally settles, his gaze fixates on me. "You've spent a millennium building walls around yourself. You've clearly worked hard at it, and I'm not asking you to tear them down for me, but I'm gonna share some chaotic insight with you."

"Please, enlighten me."

"There are people waiting on the other side whenever you're ready. And, lucky for you, I enjoy banging my head against concrete until it bleeds."

The sentiment hits harder than it should, and suddenly, my insides feel cold. It's a wave of relief, almost understanding, and for the first time in Devil knows how long, the walls feel fragile, one push away from crumbling.

Fuck, what more do I have to lose from a demon who's my carbon copy and can read me like an open book?

Despite my better judgment, I take the leap and decide to let him in.

"You're wrong, you know," I say as I stand, wiping ghoul drool off my shoulder. "I'm not the most powerful woman in the Underworld."

He sucks in a breath. "That sounded a little like humility to me."

"It's just the truth. My power means nothing in Hell —I'm just another servant, like every demon down here. This entire place reminds me of the consequences of my actions. Reality doesn't just slap me in the face; it shoves me down and stomps on my fucking throat.

"I don't have the upper hand here. I run away from my problems in the mortal world by killing, taking, and fucking the noise away. Up there, I control humans. They're useless, inconsequential bargaining chips for my survival. I'm the apex predator there. Down here? I can't kill anyone, can't touch an Underling without getting ratted out and having the Devil threaten my life.

"He and His sons have all the power over me…and I can't fucking stand it. I'm a prisoner here."

The silence stretches between us, and for a second, I regret every word. Nothing makes me feel weaker than spilling my feelings like some pathetic mortal, and I sure as Hell shouldn't have made myself small in front of an Underling. That's not who I am. That's not who I'll ever be.

When he finally speaks, the regret cuts deeper. "Spoken like a true narcissistic sociopath."

I growl. "You wanted to bang your head against my walls? I'm giving you a crack to peek through. Don't make me regret it more than I already do."

He waves his hands in surrender, stepping back. "No, no—you've got it wrong. I get you. Completely. You've spent a thousand years building a reputation, and the second you get down here, you're reminded it's all an illusion. I get it. I get *you*."

Like a true emotional roller coaster, the highs and lows make my stomach lurch. Maybe it's the softness in his voice or the way his kaleidoscope eye spins, but for whatever reason…I believe him.

I don't want to tell him he's right, but something tells me he already knows. Hell, he's called out every one of my flaws since the moment we met and never once made me feel ashamed of them—despite my prickly disposition.

When I remain silent, he twists his long, spindly finger through my platinum hair—almost exactly like the Devil does. But instead of possession and control, he does it with pure admiration. I see it in those bizarre, mismatched eyes, the way his brows soften against the exposed, torn muscle, and for a moment, his perpetual smirk fades into something sadder, gentler.

"That's the beauty of chaos—read between the lines, and the mania makes perfect sense."

I'm so lost in the raw honesty of his gaze, I completely fail to notice how close his body is to mine. Lost in the slow, lazy drift of his kaleidoscope eye, I watch as each fragment tumbles into the next, blue bleeding to purple to pink to red. Layers unfurl like rose petals in the rain, and, try as I might, I can't look away.

"Your eye is doing that thing again."

"What thing?" He tilts his head, the kaleidoscope spinning slower now, drawing me in.

"The one where…it stares…and I can't…" My words trail off as I lose myself in the twisting patterns.

"Can't what?" His voice drops to a low—dare I say seductive—timbre. His eye, that eerie mechanism meant to anchor its prey, spins in stunning patterns like snowflake fractals and geometric equations bundled with raw electricity. Just when I think I've figured them out, they shift again. "Can't what, October?"

My name on his lips hits differently than I expect, quickening my pulse. "Look away."

"Mmm," he practically purrs, closing the distance until his energy prickles across my skin. "And how does that make you feel?"

Heat pools in my stomach. "I should hate it."

"But you don't." His grin widens, showing far too many teeth. It should be terrifying. Everything about this—the realm, the circumstances, the demon—should be terrifying.

Despite it all, my breath catches. "No. I don't."

"Good." A low, predatory chuckle rumbles through his chest, laced with echoing undertones. His lips are suddenly an inch from mine. "Because I'm just getting started."

And that's when I snap out of it. My entire body erupts in goosebumps in the middle of fucking Hell, and I shiver. "Gah, how close is Cherry's realm? I feel like some of his shit is seeping through the walls."

Mayhem lets out another one of those demonic chuckles. "Debauchery? He's nowhere near here. Too prissy to slum it with the 'uglier' realms. He and Deception are sitting pretty in the upper-left quadrant, probably crimping each other's hair and getting spray tans. C'mon. Apex is just around the corner."

I force the image of the Primes into my head, brushing off the residual tension pulsing through me. But Mayhem's hypnotic eye still spins behind my eyelids, ingrained in me.

And I can't fucking shake it.

TRACK SEVEN
FEAR
YOU'RE GOING TO DIE DOWN HERE. YOU WILL ROT IN HELL AND WE WILL ALL CELEBRATE YOUR DEMISE.
YOU WILL LEARN THE TRUE MEANING OF FEAR, OCTOBER WINTERS.
WELCOME TO YOUR WORST NIGHTMARE.

TRACK SEVEN

FEAR

I'm not afraid of fear, never have been. Fear is a baseless, worthless emotion that plagues humans. They allow it to consume them because they don't know what lies beyond death, don't know that their terror is the very essence that makes them precious.

Humans are prisoners of their fear because their lives are meaningless. Finite.

My life, however, is anything but.

I do not harbor the same fears as mortals. The Primes claw at every exposed weakness, every desperate opportunity to shred my psyche, but they never succeed. Death itself wouldn't dare touch me—I've found countless ways to outsmart both it and my master.

I am still alive, still winning, despite the endless

battles and politics that threaten to strip my title and bleed me of power.

I am October fucking Winters, and I fear nothing.

The demon at my side shifts as we stand before a massive door carved from obsidian bones, his long, sinuous tail reaching for my hand—so close, I can feel the heat, yet not quite touching. Those little sparks of chaotic electricity radiating from his skin pull me from my dark musings.

Instinctively, he steps forward then hesitates, flexing those freakish knuckles that twitch like spider legs. He finally turns to face me, and the space between us crackles with unspoken tension and something that feels dangerously close to concern.

I recognize it immediately, though I've rarely seen it directed at me. He's worried about what lies beyond that door, about what it might do to me.

He's a fool to worry.

I push past him, shoving my cold hands into my jacket pockets, letting my shoulder knock against his.

"Baby, wait—"

"Don't 'baby' me," I warn him, the double entendre hitting harder than it should. "Let's just get this over with. I can't stand this fucking place, and I can't believe I'm saying this—but I miss mortals."

"Miss torturing them?" A playful smirk creeps across his impish features.

"Torturing. Killing. Raising them to do my dirty work."

"How delicious." His smirk grows into a grin. "Bet you're a fucking work of art up there, aren't you? A goddess among sheep. I could watch you burn the world for an eternity and hope to get caught in the flames."

My eyes narrow, though his words feed my famished ego—the narcissist in me who's been starving in this wretched place. "You're distracting me again."

His smile falters, replaced by that forked tongue darting across his teeth. "I'm stalling."

"Why are *you* stalling? Stalling implies avoidance, which implies worry, which is adjacent to fear. You fear nothing, remember?"

He rolls his head lazily from side to side, gazing upward as he chooses his words carefully—though I seriously doubt careful thoughts are his strong suit. "Look, I got a reputation down here."

"Congratulations, so do I—"

"—and there's a pretty good chance neither of us is walking back out that door alive."

I shrug. "They'd be stupid to kill the Devil's Second and a First of Chaos. It would start a war."

"Based on what little I've gathered from your mega-fuck-up, I'd say you already have."

There's been a lot of talk about wars during this infernal vacation, and I'm getting sick of it. I shrug again. "That's why we're going to un-fuck the fuck-up and get the fuck out of here."

"Are we a 'we' now?" There's his usual sass and that insufferable grin. I hate the effect it has on me, how, despite every logical voice in my head screaming not to fall for a demon, I deliberately ignore them all.

I press my palm against the cool obsidian door and push forward.

My heart clenches as I brace myself for impact. Though the impact of what exactly, I can't say. Another onslaught of Hellspawn and Underlings? Some gruesome torture chamber? Blood and guts everywhere? Although, when has that ever bothered me?

Mayhem's words echo in my head as we trudge forward, but my rational thoughts cut through them like a blade.

The Nightmares and Fear Primes will not kill me. They wouldn't fucking dare. They are not violent—they're sadistic. Hungry. Desperate to be fed. They do not kill, because killing their victims solves nothing except losing a mind to feed from. They need their victims alive. A dead, tortured mind is an empty vessel, and emptiness feeds no one.

We enter a chasm more expansive than the labyrinth itself, its walls covered with tangled limbs of countless souls—each one writhing and grasping for something, *anything*.

But they'll never have me.

In the center of the chasm looms a 100-foot monstrosity, weighed down by ethereal shackles, forged from some kind of blinding light. Two heads sprout from one massive body of festering muscle and twisted bone, black tendrils of smoke pouring from its exposed rib cage, forming a sea of darkness around our feet. The insects are gone now—thank fuck—but somehow, not being able to see my feet beneath these dark clouds feels even more unsettling.

The shackles clang against their shared body as they slowly crane their twin heads upward from their sullen state, fixing their gaze upon me.

The entire chasm trembles with the sound of their booming words.

"October Winters," the eerie, dual-voiced Nightmares and Fear Prime hisses my name like a curse.

"Sup, creeps." I nod at them, feigning nonchalance while every atom in my body seizes with utter dread. I'm a speck of dust compared to them, something they could flick off their shoulder without a second thought.

Despite the physical disparity, I outrank them tenfold.

Let's just hope they play fair.

"You are not welcome here," Nightmares rumbles, his voice strained against the chains binding his throat. "How did you gain access to our realm?"

"That would be my doing." Mayhem steps forward,

tail lowered, horns dipping as he bows his head in submission.

"First of Chaos," they speak in unison. "How dare you defy our authority."

He waves his hand dismissively. "S'not a defiance at all, your terror-ful-ness." I smirk at the nickname. "I've brought her here as an offering." I open my mouth to protest the ever-loving shit out of my so-called escort, but he continues his little song and dance. "She's going to break your curse."

The massive heads turn toward each other, some silent communication passing between them. When they look back at me, there's something predatory in their gaze. "And how does she propose to do that?" Fear's voice carries a note of bitter resentment.

"Curse breaking 101." I find myself making yet another quip. "My necromancy can unbind spectral chains. Just need a few souls to power me up. You've got plenty down here for me to draw from."

"These souls are ours by right—you shall not consume them," they speak, their rumbling voices shaking the ground. "You've already stolen one from us." Their gaze fixes on my finger.

Ah, yes. I haven't forgotten. The Mark they left on my ex-lover-turned-familiar.

"This curse cannot be broken by necromancy," Nightmares's low, trembling voice speaks. "It requires something far stronger."

Fear continues: "Divine magic binds us here; a Divine soul will release us." Black tendrils stretch from their bones, reaching toward my hand. "Specifically, one of the souls who helped put us here."

Reality hits me like a sledgehammer to the chest. The color drains from my face, blood racing through my heart as it struggles to keep up its frantic rhythm. "No," I whisper. "You can't have him."

"His soul belonged to us," Fear hisses, voice dripping with venom. "Rightfully ours. Not only did you steal from us, you aided him in our imprisonment." A massive skeletal hand lifts one of the gargantuan shackles for emphasis.

"His soul is *mine*," I snarl. "Granted to me by Lucifer himself. He's my familiar now. Consuming his soul would destroy half of mine. And destroying me is *not* in your best interest."

Twin sets of black eyes narrow in cold scrutiny. "So it would seem."

Fuck. My organs continue to twist and writhe in agony, desperation pooling like acid in my stomach. I recall just weeks ago—or however long it's been in this timeless Hell—when Lovejoy and I discovered the ritual remnants beneath the demonic hub in Hollywood Hills. Occultist, Nephilim, Prime. Three ingredients for the perfect sacrifice.

It's no secret that consuming Nephilim essence strengthens a Prime's hold on the mortal realm. I'd discovered that little tidbit when I overheard that pixie bitch Mireya muttering it to Lovejoy the day I delivered her back into his arms.

Trapping a Nephilim in Hell was a faultless punishment for the Divine fucks. The ultimate torture. But it never occurred to me that consuming his soul would undo this curse.

All at once, the gears click into place.

And everything makes terrible sense.

"Purity is the ultimate curse breaker." I step forward, pacing the expanse. "A pure, Divine soul would grant your release and give you full access to the mortal realm. But here's what you fail to grasp, in all your infinite wisdom." My sadistic grin spreads across my face as I pause for dramatic effect. "Declan Lovejoy's soul would be utterly useless to you. His soul is anything but pure. I made damn sure of that. There was darkness in him that I—*and only I*—cultivated. Your Mark means nothing compared to my corruption. Consuming a tainted Nephilim soul wouldn't save you—it would poison you from within."

The silence is so suffocating, so deadly, that for a moment, I'm certain the entire chasm will collapse in on itself. The twins' weary but furious gazes bore into me, and for a split second, I glance at Mayhem, who stands with arms folded across his chest, eyes darting between the Primes and me like he's watching a death match.

Finally, I break the silence. "His soul was always meant to be mine. You can never have him."

Four black eyes hold me, unblinking, merciless, weighing me with eternity. "Then you will bring us another."

I suck in a breath. There is only one other Nephilim I know of, wretched as he may be. The little fucker who got away. The one I swore I'd destroy the second I got the chance. What better way to ruin him than having him consumed by the very Prime who swore to devour his mentor?

It's the ideal solution.

Rid the world of another demon hunter. Break the curse. Stop the war before it starts. Repair the fractured relationship with my master.

He will be so proud of me.

The smile tugging at my lips couldn't be more twisted.

"Fine," I grit out through bared teeth. "I will bring you another."

I spin on my heels to face Mayhem and the door, but the twins' haunting voices halt me.

"Not so fast, witch." I look over my shoulder to see one of their skeletal hands reaching out for me. "We must bind our oath. A life for a life. A soul for a soul."

I've never made a binding contract with a Prime before. I'm not that fucking stupid, and I certainly wouldn't take an oath over something I'm not capable of completing.

But Jehovah…Jeronimo…whatever the fuck his name is has to be dealt with.

And this is the only way.

"I accept," I declare, my voice ringing clearly through the chasm.

Within seconds, smoke pours from inside their rib cage, flowing like a sinister river toward me. It circles me, threatening to suffocate me before finding my left hand to seal our pact.

But the tendril recoils violently the moment it touches my hand.

The entire chasm begins to tremble.

Instinctively, my head whips around to find Mayhem. A desperate need to grab him and ensure we aren't separated in this godforsaken place roils in my stomach. But the ground continues to quake. Cracks split around me in a perfect circle until I'm suspended on an isolated platform not unlike the Ring of the Thirteen.

"You murdered our children," Nightmares roars, and the souls trapped in the walls begin to shriek, limbs thrashing wildly. "In *our* domain."

Fuck. Fuck fuck fuck.

They sense the demons I stored in Lovejoy.

"They got in my way." I fight against the dread clawing through my core, something eerily akin to fear spreading through my veins like poison. The twins crawl closer, their spectral chains clanging loudly.

"Did you think you could hide the truth from us, foolish witch?" Fear hisses. "Did you forget the soul bound in that ring is still one we can hear? Our Mark is forever, even after death." He releases a breathy, sickening chuckle. "It seems even a creature soul-bound to you will betray you."

I look at my scorpion ring and clench my jaw. "He has a talent for that."

The monstrous Primes nearly double in size, and I've never felt smaller. Their voices deepen, raw with guttural anguish, as the walls begin to close in. Panic coils around my throat, and those outstretched hands of the trapped souls seize me.

Hundreds of decrepit hands dig into my skin, their sharp claws tearing at my jacket, threatening to rip me apart.

I try to blast them with fire magic, but the Primes' power is too great. I'm trapped, a prisoner of their fury.

Nightmares and Fear are not violent. They will not kill me. The Devil would never allow it.

"You're going to die down here." The voices from the labyrinth roar in my ears—I can't tell if it's these souls or just memories haunting me on repeat. "You will rot in Hell, October Winters, and we will all celebrate your demise."

I can't breathe. I can't fucking breathe.

The dark tendrils circle me again, black smoke flooding my nostrils, ears, and eyes. Fear's shrill voice shreds through my skull, ripping the air from my chest as darkness devours my sight.

"You will learn the true meaning of fear, October Winters."

My knees buckle, my body betraying me as I collapse. Behind the roaring in my ears, Nightmares's gravelly voice reverberates through my very soul:

"Welcome to your worst nightmare."

TRACK EIGHT
WELCOME TO MY NIGHTMARE

THE ACRID STENCH OF BURNING WOOD, ASH, AND scorched stone assaults my nostrils, dragging me back to consciousness.

My body is swathed in heavy sheep's wool, the coarse fibers scratching my skin as I struggle to throw it off. Heat surrounds me, angry and merciless. Smoke claws at my lungs, poisoning what little air remains. I finally kick the wool away, scrambling to my feet to take in my surroundings.

But all I see are flames.

Flames that aren't mine.

Flames that sear my flesh as they lick my skin.

Within the flames, I can make out a wooden cottage, its furnishings crumbling to ash. There's something achingly familiar about the layout—the small windows, the vaulted ceilings, the straw thatching now burning to cinders. I long to look out the window, to see what lies beyond this inferno, but the flames are too vicious, too deadly.

It's the first time fire has ever hurt me.

And I can't escape it.

"Mayhem?" I call out, but my voice emerges as a warbled rasp. I search frantically for my demonic escort, coughing as ash and embers choke me, as wooden beams crash from the ceiling, threatening to crush me. But he's nowhere to be found.

No chaos. No electricity crackling through the air. No one.

No one but me and flames that hunger to destroy me.

I leap aside when a burning banister crashes at my feet. The floorboards groan beneath me, shrieking like something in agony. I flinch at every sound, terror coiling around my heart in strangling vines.

I try to remind myself they're not Underlings. It's just my weight. The floor can't hurt me.

Can it?

"I'm not going to fucking die here," I snarl through the smoke. "I haven't survived this long to be taken out by some nightmare."

That's what this is. A nightmare. A living nightmare.

I stumble past burning wood, desperate to find an exit. I press the crook of my arm to my nose, shielding myself from the smoke, and shriek when an ember strikes my cheek. The skin burns like nothing I've ever felt—blistering and spreading until my entire cheek goes numb. I bring my hand to the wound and then recoil in horror at what I see.

They're…smaller. Needle-tipped claws, tiny hands bubbled with boils. Red flesh swirling into orange.

I stare down at my hands and choke back the wail clawing up my throat.

The room towers above me now, as if I've shrunk to the size of a child's doll. I try to scream, to speak, but instead, my voice emerges as a high-pitched squeak—and the words aren't English.

They're Hellspeak.

Jesus fucking Christ.

I've been turned into a Hellspawn.

It's the perfect manifestation of what the twins believe to be my deepest terror—utter powerlessness. Slavery. I'm a small, pathetic creature lost in a sea of countless others just like me. No power, no status, just another attention-starved thing begging for scraps of praise from Lesser Underlings who wouldn't spare me a glance.

My breath catches in my tiny chest when a figure enters the burning cottage—tall and imposing despite the linen rags kissed by flames. It's a woman, beautiful but menacing. Her hazel eyes blaze in the firelight, blonde braids cascading over her shoulders. But as she steps closer, I realize there isn't just one head of golden hair.

There are two.

"Abomination," she snarls, staring at my pathetic form with disgust—and that's when recognition slams into me.

My mother stands before me, twin-headed with razor-sharp teeth dripping black, demonic ichor.

This *is* a fucking nightmare. A twisted, horrific perversion of the memory the twins fed from just days ago. My pathetic Hellspawn brain can barely process the reality—all it wants is to run, to hide, to cower from this monstrous thing hurling venom at me.

But as the two-headed form of my mother draws closer, her voice begins to shift higher. Shriller. More familiar.

"Your soul is laid bare to us, October Winters," Fear's voice echoes, each word scraping down my spine like nails on a chalkboard.

"You cannot hide the truth from us in our own realm," the other head, Nightmares, continues. Their voices weave into something that makes my bones ache with dread. "We see every festering wound in your wretched, black heart."

The Primes' forms begin to shift, morphing from the monstrous version of my mother into something smaller. A young, petite female—maybe 20 or 25 at most

—with a face almost a perfect mirror of my own features.

But it's not me.

It's so much fucking worse.

Terror floods my veins like poison, seeping into me until I can't move, can't breathe, can't think straight. Every nightmare scenario crashes through my mind at once. I try to retrace my steps—the past year, the past few days. It's impossible. I left her body in Vegas a year ago, soulless and still. The shaman confirmed it the other day. No change, no hope.

She can't be here.

But I can't look away. Not from her. The one soul I wouldn't deliver. The one that started this whole goddamn mess. The one that led me from mistake to mistake until I landed in Hell, facing the impossible with everything on the line.

She has his eyes, those intense, dark brown eyes that followed me for 80 years. Eyes I was certain I'd never see again. But there they are, just as soul-consuming as her father's. And what's worse? There are two sets of them.

Two heads, like my mother's form before, mirror the same face. Elegant features reveal my own bloodline, crowned with the dark locks she inherited from *him*. She is her father in every way that matters, but she's a perfect, devastating mixture of us both. And I cannot bear to face her for another second.

But her voice…

That's what will haunt me forever.

"Mother."

The word shatters me. My legs collapse like splintered toothpicks, and I don't even care that I'm sinking into a rotting wooden floor. The flames might as well not exist. All I see is her.

The girl who called herself Eve.

"How does it feel, Mother?" the thing wearing Lovejoy's and my daughter's face asks, and the mere mention of the word sends bile rising in my throat. Fuck, how I wish she were a ghost. Those, I can dismiss with a wave of my hand. This, I can't. "How does it feel to face what your failures created? Can you live with yourself? Can you stand knowing you destroyed so many lives—*destroyed mine*—to ensure your own miserable existence continues?"

They're using Lovejoy's words—his exact fucking words—against me. A conversation so recent, it's still ringing in my ears despite every effort to forget it. I'm a prisoner in my own mind, logic desperately whispering that this is just the twins' twisted game, that she's not real. But still.

Hearing his cruelty in her voice makes it feel like gospel.

The two-headed apparition of my 20-year-old daughter reaches for my throat, her fingers and thumb closing around the pudgy flesh and lifting me to her eye level.

Her eyes are *exactly* like his.

Haunting, dark, and full of hatred.

"He wanted me because He grew tired of you." The heads speak in unison, her sweet voice dripping with malice. "He wanted a new Second. Someone more powerful. Someone born of Heaven and Hell who could rule by His side and bring the world to its knees. You couldn't do that. You couldn't even deliver Him a thousand souls in six days."

How could they know? How could these fucking terror twins know *any* of this? Of her? My best-kept secret, one I swore I'd never tell another soul?

Are her words just echoes of the fears I harbored when I discovered who she really was a year and a half ago? Are the twins so deep in my psyche that they're ripping out every anxious thought, every nightmare I've tried to bury?

This can't be real.

Eve isn't real.

I left her body in Las Vegas and hid her soul where no one could ever find it.

Not even Him.

Something in her features begins to shift then. Her eyes remain the same while her cheeks and jaw broaden into a more masculine shape, stubble sprouting across the skin. Within seconds, the body stretches taller, taking a male form.

Lovejoy.

"I'll follow you forever, October Winters. To Hell and back, if that's what it takes. And I will make every second of it your ultimate torture."

Their form shifts again, but this transformation is more grotesque than all the others. The two-headed apparition splits, erupting in a black, chitinous exoskeleton covered in coarse hair. Each head morphs into massive, clicking claws, eight legs bursting from the sides. A massive tail curves overhead, its bulbous stinger pulsing with sickening golden light: filled with souls.

The twins have taken the form of Nero. A bear-sized emperor scorpion, poised to strike. Ready to devour.

I'm helpless to move, anchored to the burning floor where I first awoke. The gargantuan scorpion scuttles toward me, snapping razor-sharp claws that could sever my head in one snap. I try to scream, but no sound escapes. My tiny heart lodges in my throat as the monster's stinger coils back and strikes like lightning, piercing my eye right where the ember burned me.

The agony is beyond comparison. I wonder if I'll ever escape this fucking nightmare.

But through the searing pain, I hear something impossible—a voice that doesn't belong in this nightmare. Distant, like muffled music from a gramophone. Calling my name. Getting closer.

The scorpion's form begins to flicker, its golden light dimming.

"October, wake up!"

And then, the entire nightmare explodes into fragments of shadow and smoke.

A sharp inhale tears through me as air floods back into my lungs.

I scramble to feel my surroundings, only to shriek when I touch cool dirt crawling with insects. They form a perfect circle around me, as if some invisible barrier is keeping them from swarming over my body. My hands frantically search myself—the familiar cool leather of my jacket, the torn threads in my dark jeans, the choker around my throat. Platinum blonde hair spills through my peripheral vision, cascading past my shoulders to rest above my chest.

I'm out of the nightmare. I'm alive. I'm still me.

"Easy there, kitten," the familiar, chaotic voice pulls me from my panic.

My eyes find him—my demonic escort. The Chaos

demon with mismatched eyes and curling horns and that absolutely trashy-yet-sexy outfit.

"Mayhem." His name escapes my lips like an unholy prayer. "Are you real? Please be real. Please don't be another nightmare—"

"I'm real." He pulls me against his chest, his voice rough with something that might be relief. "Look at me."

My exhausted, burning eyes find his—those horribly mismatched eyes. The nauseating kaleidoscope and black void have never looked so beautiful, so familiar.

"How did you find me?" I whisper, my voice cracking.

"Ate my way through the nightmare refrigerator." His grin is feral, satisfied.

I blink hard, trying to process. "Wait—seriously?"

"I was hungry." He shrugs with mock casualness, but his hands shake slightly as he wipes my tears away with his thumbs. The tremor proves he's real— my nightmares would never show me his vulner- ability.

The ambient glow of the Nightmare and Fear portal illuminates his face in haunting ways. We're still inside their realm, but we're at the start of the labyrinth. Away from the Apex, from the Nightmare Wing—which I am certain I was just stuck in—and away from the Primes. Cool dread sets in when I realize he must have clawed his way out of the Nightmare Wing with me, betraying every ounce of trust Nightmares and Fear may have ever had in him.

"The twins, they'll—"

"Yeah, they're not gonna be happy with me. Will probably revoke my permissions to enter their realm." His kaleidoscope eye spins faster, betraying his anxiety. "But I don't give a shit. My job was to protect you. I wasn't going to let them break you." His voice drops, fierce and possessive. "That's my job."

A broken laugh croaks out of me. "I've never been more grateful for your terrible flirting than I am right now."

"Hey, I'm insulted." He crushes me against his chest, and I feel the mesh of his shirt against my cheek, solid and real. "My flirting is an art form."

I bury my face in him. "Get used to the insults. They're *my* art form."

"Wouldn't want it any other way, you beautiful disaster."

Our closeness, this impossible intimacy, is something I've only ever shared with the Devil—and in many ways, Lovejoy. It lays my heart bare for him to devour. It's raw, unforgiving, completely untethered from logic or self-preservation. A mindfuck I'll never recover from.

Mayhem knows my nightmares. He's seen my deepest fears, and he saved me despite them.

But somewhere beneath this façade of tenderness lies duty—loyalty to his Prime, to Lucifer. I can't fight the anguish twisting in my chest, the bitter certainty that this is all a performance, one designed to pacify his master and mine.

He isn't here because he cares about me.

He's here because he has a job to do.

So why does his touch feel so goddamn real?

I look up at him, studying the monstrous teeth, mismatched eyes, exposed muscle, and torn features. For a moment, I forget he's a demon. I forget he's as unstable and sadistic as I am, that he revels in pain and watches chaos unfold with the same twisted pleasure I do. He truly is my dark reflection.

Just a lot less pretty.

Our mouths are mere inches apart, our breaths mingling as I lean closer to the demonic façade that should terrify me. Instead, I find myself drawn to the danger he represents—to the way his kaleidoscope eye seems to see straight through every wall I've built, every wall he tries to bang his head against.

Heat pools low in my stomach as our lips inch closer…

But I'm jolted from my spiraling thoughts when a thunderous boom echoes through the labyrinth. Mayhem instinctively pulls me behind him, his lithe, muscular frame towering over me as those spindly fingers flex, prepared for battle.

Teal-blue light bleeds into my peripheral vision. A haunting mist solidifies as it rounds a corner, ethereal shackles clanging in the distance as their owner spins them like a whip ready to strike. With it comes the hum of that gravelly, dark melody that once commanded the stage on Halloween night.

"Oh, come the fuck on," Mayhem and I groan in perfect unison—the ideal response to yet another inevitable clusterfuck.

Here we fucking go.

TRACK NINE
MY OWN SUMMER
(SHOVE IT)

TRACK NINE

MY OWN SUMMER (SHOVE IT)

Summer Jones is a vision of death incarnate, a ghostly apparition wreathed in spectral chains and lethal intent. The eerie echo of her death-song crackles at the edges like charred parchment, a voice that rasps and scrapes rather than sings. She sings the same haunting melody I heard as I climbed the stage to face the Devil possessing her. Now, though, her powerful form is twisted into something far more sinister.

She stands before us, spinning those chains like an unforgiving carnival ride, a twisted grin spreading across her features that rivals my demonic escort's.

Mayhem steps forward without hesitation, forked tongue sliding across his grotesque lips as his towering frame moves to intercept her. I immediately grab his shoulder, yanking him back to step in front of him.

"Hold your horses, buddy. You don't want this drive-thru special."

He releases a dark chuckle. "Says you. I'm still starving."

"She's mine to handle."

"Am I?" Summer tilts her head with predatory curiosity.

"Surprised you didn't get absorbed into the walls," I reply, lifting my chin and flashing her a cold smirk. "Guess you're not worthy of a permanent spot in the labyrinth either."

Her low, bone-chilling laugh sends ice through my veins, but I refuse to show weakness. She sneers, "How ironic that you consider yourself the arbiter of worthiness. You're nothing down here, October Winters."

"Aw, did the creepy wall voices tell you that? You should have seen what I did to them for pissing me off."

She lunges forward with supernatural speed—one second ten feet away, the next behind me, chains wrapping around my throat. They can't suffocate me literally, but the spectral magic coursing through them burns my skin like acid. She spins us around, slamming my body against the labyrinth walls, where skeletal hands burst forth to seize every limb, anchoring me in their bone-white grip. She yanks her chains tighter, and my hands flail desperately, fingers crackling with fire magic in one hand, death magic in the other. If I could just break free, I could siphon her soul. Rules be damned—I'd be rid of her, and we could escape this nightmare.

I force a hissing laugh against her chains. "You're new down here, so I'll let this slide. But killing me isn't in your best interest, Jones."

"Who said anything about killing you?" She bares spectral teeth. "I want you suffering down here with me for eternity."

"There are better ways to make friends."

"You and I will never be friends." She tightens the chains until I wince, but I lift my chin in defiance. The skeletal hands grip my wrists harder, and my instinct screams at me to awaken Lovejoy, send him crawling up their arms to strike with his venomous stinger.

But I can't rely on my familiar anymore, and I'm far too weak to force him into submission.

Weak.

I've never been weak. Not truly. I've been outsmarted, overpowered, but when the world turns against me, I remind it exactly who's in charge.

Weakness has been my downfall in Hell. I've been the Primes' punching bag for too long. It's time to reclaim my power.

I summon whatever strength remains. I don't need my hands—I have the darkness within me to send this bitch flying.

"Restless spirit who will not quit,

Loosen your chains as I see fit,

Burn by wrath upon my pyre,
Light this fucking place on fire."

My flames erupt from within, and the walls shriek as they burn. Fire kisses my skin like a lover's caress as Summer reels back, falling straight onto her ass. She lifts her head, midnight hair floating in ethereal waves around her ghostly skull. She releases a monstrous snarl and rises just as I break free from my bonds.

But before she can advance, she's yanked backward.

Mayhem clamps his hand around her throat.

He spins her to face him, studying her with intensity —but the ravenous hunger has vanished from his eyes. He doesn't devour her like the others. His jaw remains intact, teeth clamped shut. She thrashes against his grip, ghostly feet kicking while her aura pulses with fury. But he overpowers her easily. She's just a spirit—nothing against a high-level demon.

My breath catches when her struggles begin to weaken. He draws her face closer to his until I'm certain their lips will meet.

They never do.

He simply stares.

Stares the way he stares at me.

I know what it's like to be caught in Mayhem's hypnotic gaze. To lose yourself in those spinning fractals that bleed every color imaginable. To surrender all rational thought to his consuming power meant to devour and destroy. He never fully ensnared me because he chose restraint.

But Summer Jones is not as lucky.

I move on shaky feet to watch the exchange from a better angle and become trapped in the hypnotic marvel of watching the First of Chaos unleash his most terrifying power. His razor-sharp claws pierce her chest, sinking into the translucent edges of her exposed ribs and locking her against him like a vise. Her powerful, muscular frame goes completely slack in his grip as she becomes ensnared by the kaleidoscope eye. It spins in slow, mesmerizing spirals that drag her consciousness deeper with each rotation, rendering her utterly helpless.

All the while, I watch his void-like eye begin to devour her sanity. Teal-blue wisps of her very essence tear from her skull like smoke, streaming into that bottomless black pit with wet, sucking sounds that make my stomach churn. Her spectral form flickers and convulses as he drains piece after piece of her mind, her mouth opening in a silent scream that never comes.

That's when the insects begin to swarm up her body.

And with them come black, demonic tendrils belonging to the Nightmares and Fear Primes themselves.

Mayhem is lost to his own power, trapped in his entrancing magic, draining every fragment of her sanity until she begins withering into nothing. But the insects and tendrils multiply, crawling into her exposed rib cage, skittering beneath what remains of her translucent skin like writhing tumors. It's revolting—bile burns up my throat, acidic and choking, but I can't tear my eyes away.

That's when I realize it isn't just any swarm invading her corporeal form. It's one species in particular.

Milkweed beetles, blue and shimmering with otherworldly iridescence.

They're the symbols of transformation. Resilience. Rebirth.

As the tendrils coil tighter around her dissolving form, the truth slams into me like a physical blow: she's transforming.

I have to move. I need to stop this before it's too late. With every passing second, her spirit fractures, but the demonic magic saturating this realm has different plans for Summer Jones.

The Nightmares and Fear Primes speak directly into my mind, their power slicing through my mental defenses. They aren't tormenting me with fears—they're delivering a promise.

"She will haunt you forever, October Winters." The two voices invade my skull in unison. *"You may have escaped us, but you will never escape her. You will bring us a Nephilim soul, and she will ensure it. Fail our bargain, and she will drag you back to us so we can obliterate you for good."*

Over my immortal dead body, you sadistic fucks.

I don't give a damn that killing demons is forbidden. The worst has already come from breaking that rule. Despite every twisted law, despite the ridiculous politics enforced by the Primes and their Father, I don't care anymore. What more can they possibly take from me?

Mayhem risked everything to save me from the Nightmare Wing. I'll risk everything to save him from the monster I created.

The Devil's wrath is tomorrow's problem.

I position myself behind Summer, hovering my hands over her skull. The smoky tendrils recoil like startled serpents, but I blast them away with raw, necromantic force. The beetles continue burrowing into her spectral form, slowly restoring her strength, so I focus everything I have on siphoning her soul into my grasp.

The battle between Mayhem's hypnotic gaze, the Primes, and my magic becomes an infernal tug-of-war that threatens to shatter my already fragile mind. I struggle against the writhing tendrils, against the invasive beetles, when the twins' voices slice through my consciousness like razors.

"We know your deepest, most shameful secret, October Winters, and we will wield it as our weapon until you honor our bargain. You discovered your own flesh and blood, your precious daughter, and you stole her soul for yourself rather than deliver it to our Father as commanded. You did so out of pure jealousy and spite, knowing He could only want her for

one reason: because she is everything you are not. Because she can give Him what you never could. You are expendable to Him, October Winters, and you will rot in our domain for eternity when He's finished with you."

The truth obliterates me.

No one has ever known what I truly did. Not the full scope of it. No one knows about Eve, or the despicable, unforgivable acts I committed to ensure I remained the Devil's favorite. It's that fear and selfishness that define me, that created this rotten creature fueled by darkness, sadism, and pure corruption.

Eve was meant to be my best-kept secret.

And now, she belongs to them.

My unholy scream tears through the realm like a sonic weapon, shattering both Mayhem's hypnotic hold and my necromantic grip on Summer. We crash to the ground, helpless as her form solidifies before our eyes—translucent skin stretching over exposed bone, dead flesh knitting itself together while blazing white eyes illuminate a corpse-pale face. The tendrils and beetles vanish, leaving her reborn into something far worse than death.

She is alive again but still utterly dead.

And her demonic growl freezes my blood.

Necromancy. Mania. Corruption. Rage.

The ideal ingredients for a catastrophic demise.

Summer's scream deafens us then. Not the wail of a banshee—this is the death-cry of a freshly sired demonic creature of the Nightmares and Fear Broodline, a being that can traverse realms, human and infernal alike. She speaks only a single word.

"Go."

Within seconds, the entire realm erupts in ear-splitting wails of the damned. Mayhem seizes my hand, dragging me toward the glowing portal that's opened for our escape. He urges me forward, pulling me through the gate, and the bitter truth follows.

We've created a monster, a rock star poltergeist born from the catalyst of my hubris.

And she will haunt me unless I pay for my catastrophic mistakes.

USE YOUR CHAOS ON ME. SCRAMBLE MY BRAIN UNTIL THERE'S NOTHING FUCKING LEFT.
FEAR IS JUST ANOTHER THING TO BURN, SO LIGHT THE MATCH. THAT'S WHAT THE DEVIL'S FUCKING SECOND WOULD DO.
TRACK TEN
HEART-SHAPED BOX

TRACK TEN

HEART-SHAPED BOX

The screaming finally stops. It feels like hours of it —the shrieks of the dead, Summer's last wail, my own voice threatening to break—and now, there's nothing but silence.

Cold stone bites into my cheek as I fall face-first onto the ground. I spit a mouthful of blood onto the platform and force myself upright, blinking until my vision clears. A dozen Gothic archways greet me, each one pulsing with eerie essences and Hellspeak inscriptions that glow with Hellish light. Behind me, the arch to the Nightmare and Fear Realm still writhes with movement.

We're back at the Ring of the Thirteen. We escaped the wrath of the twins. I wish I could say I'm met with the warm embrace of relief, but I'm far from it. Nowhere fucking close.

Bile rises in my throat as my stomach churns

violently. I tear the black choker from my neck and rip off my leather jacket, tossing both aside. I can still feel them crawling all over me—the spiders, the ants, the beetles. Especially the fucking beetles.

I can't shake what we just witnessed. What we did. Summer's transformation, the insects swarming her spirit, burrowing into her essence until she became something beyond corporeal but miles away from alive. I can still hear them tearing at her ghostly flesh, still see her body convulsing as the insects burrowed beneath her skin and Nightmares and Fear's power flooded in.

Mayhem and I created a monster. And while it may be over, this isn't the last we'll see of Summer Jones.

A jolt of panic shoots through me when my demonic escort appears in my peripheral vision, crawling on his hands and knees like some ravenous Hellspawn. Every hair on my body stands on end as my fingers curl, fire magic crackling at my fingertips, ready to strike.

He raises his hands in surrender. "Hey, hey, whoa— it's just me, babe."

I release an exasperated breath, shooting him a look so murderous, it could make Hell seem like a vacation. But instead of backing away, he leans closer.

"Huh. Would you look at that." A curious grin reaches his demonic eyes. "We match now."

"What?" The word scrapes from my throat.

"Your eye. Must have burst something during that last spell."

Ice floods through me as I scramble for my jacket, clawing through pockets for my athame. In the blade's reflective surface, I see what Mayhem's referring to: my left iris blazes fire-engine red instead of my usual hazel, like fresh blood has replaced the color entirely. Tiny black veins crawl across my lid and cheekbone like infected capillaries.

"Fuck," I snarl, my stomach lurching. "They Marked me."

"The twins?"

"Yeah. They did it in the Nightmare Wing. I just…I didn't realize that's what it was." I run my hands over my face, but the sting of the Mark causes me to wince. "They'll always be able to find me now. They'll hunt me down with that fucking rock star poltergeist until it's all done. Until I give them exactly what they need to…" My words trail as I drive my boot into the ancient stone, cursing as the impact echoes. "They know. They fucking *know* about her. And now *you* know. No one else can know. I've lost too much—"

The emotions slam into me like a tidal wave: fear, frustration, grief, guilt, absolute fucking panic. Images of Summer's transformation dissolve into visions of Eve —her face, her voice, her father's cruel words spilling from her lips. All at once, she's in front of me again, threatening to take my place as the Devil's Second, threatening to destroy me.

I reach for my ear instinctively, but my chest caves

when I realize the earring isn't there. It's a ring now—a perfect black loop with a scorpion nestled on my finger.

But he isn't Nero. He isn't my familiar.

He's a monument to every fucking failure I've ever made.

The pain burrows into my bones, taking root deeper than it ever has.

Finally, I shatter.

"Mayhem." My voice cracks like glass, and I fucking hate myself for it. That eerie, kaleidoscope eye searches me, dissecting every broken piece. "I need you to make me forget. Kiss me."

His brows furrow, confusion flickering across his face like he's trying to decode whether I mean Demon-Kiss or something else entirely. I crawl closer, my hands shaking against the stone. "Your eyes. Use your chaos on me. Scramble my brain until there's nothing fucking left."

The kaleidoscope stops spinning. For the first time since I've known him, Mayhem's grin dies completely, and those razor-sharp teeth disappear behind pressed lips. "No."

"What the fuck do you mean, 'no'?" The words tear from my throat as I fight the sob building in my chest.

"I won't Kiss you, October." His voice is softer than I've ever heard it, void of its sing-song, patronizing melody, and somehow that makes it worse. "I won't let you run from what we saw back there. You need to remember every second of it." His long, spindly fingers touch my trembling hands, and, for once, I don't flinch away. "Fear is just another thing to burn, so light the match. That's what the Devil's fucking Second would do."

His words hit me like a brick, but I'm too tired to fight him.

"I know why you run, babe." His thumb traces my knuckles before stopping right above my ring finger. I slam my eyes shut, but the memory slices through me anyway. Lovejoy's accusations and every cruel jab ever made about my cowardice cut at me like glass in my chest. I don't need another man dissecting me, telling me who I am and what to feel without even fucking knowing me.

Not now. Not ever.

But Mayhem's voice cuts through the noise in my head. "You jump from one job to the next, burying yourself in violence to avoid the agony you've got locked away. You get drunk on the chaos because it drowns out everything else. I don't fucking blame you—it's intoxicating. Believe me, I know. Living so wildly, you keep your past from catching up." His grip tightens on my hand. "But that pain is rotting you from the inside out. You need to mourn what you lost. Until you do, you'll destroy yourself more than my Kiss ever could." Finally, his fingers find my scorpion ring and twist it off. Every instinct screams to snatch it back, but I stop myself. He's not Nero.

"If you want to forget, I'll help you." Mayhem's voice drops to barely a whisper. "But not like that."

It's the dumbest act of kindness I've seen from a demon in centuries. And fuck me, I want to kiss his stupid disaster of a mouth.

I lose all rational thought as I grab him by the collar and crash my lips to his. It's awkward at first—the left side of his mouth surprisingly soft while the other scrapes against my skin, his sharp, exposed teeth threatening to draw blood. There's hunger and chaos as his kiss claims me, his entire being pulling me in like I'm a precious meal. I taste copper on his tongue, and the metallic sensation sets my skin ablaze.

It should be horrifying, the most unsettling, fucked-up kiss of my life.

And yet…I've never wanted anything more.

For a moment, I forget everything—but reality crashes back when he pulls away.

"Wait," he whispers against my lips.

"Really?" I groan. "You've been eye-fucking me since we met, and *now* you're backing out?"

"Don't get your panties in a twist, kitten." He chuckles as he rubs his hands together. "Just making good on one of your rules."

I tilt my head, eyes narrowing as his long fingers trail up his forehead and over his horns, down his neck and across his arms. In seconds, his demonic skin melts away, morphing into an earthy tan covered in intricate tattoos. His hair levels into a perfect quiff with a sharp part on the left, right where his monstrous grin had stretched. And his eyes…eyes that were once a chaotic marvel now stare back at me as heterochromatic orbs. One green, swirled with blue, mimicking a kaleidoscope, and the other dark brown. There's still that hint of mischief dancing in them. He's still Mayhem, still him in that cropped leather jacket and fishnet shirt.

"You could have spared me the eyesore this whole time." I shoot him a playful smirk. "You're not too bad to look at like this."

"Not all Broodlines can throw on human glamours in Hell at the drop of a hat." He shrugs, almost bashful. "Mine hasn't quite mastered that yet. Figured I'd give it my best shot for you."

A sharp clang pierces the air as Mayhem hurls my ring toward the arches. My eyes track its path obsessively as it skitters across stone, bouncing past each portal until it finally settles against the base of a distant arch.

Mayhem's fingers find my belt loops, pulling me closer as he inhales my scent. His hips are flush with my abdomen, digging his hard length against me. I grasp his hands, tugging at the black gloves until his fingers are free. I trail mine across his arms, marveling at how the scars have shifted into dark tattoos that echo the same geometric patterns. His palm finds the back of my neck and pulls me close to him as his lips kiss from my collarbone to my ear. Leaning my head back with a contented sigh, I melt into his touch.

Silence is a welcome gift right now. All I hear are the quiet hitches in his breath, the small rumblings of seductive chuckles, and satisfied hums echoing throughout the platform.

I don't care that any demon could walk out of any gate at any moment. Maybe that's part of the thrill. The recklessness. The way danger consumes me like Hellfire.

Or maybe I just don't give a fuck anymore.

And speaking of the fucks I've run out of…

My eyes find my ring again, where it lies alone near the Nightmare and Fear arch. Fitting. Too fitting.

I stretch my hand outward, fingers wriggling lazily as I whisper my familiar's awakening spell.

In seconds, the ring transforms into a scorpion. Immediately, the erratic, jumbled thoughts of my ex-lover fill my mind, but he isn't concerned with me just yet. He panics over his surroundings, claws clicking and tail curling. He searches for a place to hide, a shadow to conceal himself in. I know he can't see us from this far away—not with his poor vision—but I know he can hear me. Hear *us*.

I curl the fingers of my outstretched hand inward and mutter another spell, one that anchors my little scorpion to the hot floor, unable to move, unable to shield himself from us.

And for the first time since it all happened, I turn his voice off.

It's as easy as flipping a light switch, something I knew I had in me but couldn't reach. My inner demons were just too loud. But now, with the help of a little chaos, I silence those too.

I take my power back.

"There," I say, voice low and venomous, dripping with satisfaction. "Now you're just like that pathetic apprentice of yours."

Mayhem chuckles against my neck when I return to the middle of the platform, kissing and sucking at the sensitive skin under my ear. "You magnificent little psychopath. You're making him watch."

"He fucking deserves it." My eyes never leave the scorpion.

Mayhem hooks his fingers under the straps of my tank top and drags them down my shoulders. He hunches to accommodate our height difference, his tongue tracing a slow path from my ear to my chest before he pulls the fabric down further. Despite Hell's brutal heat, goosebumps ripple across my skin. His touch crackles, electric and alive, the chaotic energy making my body react in ways the infernal warmth never could.

He worships my breasts like a man dying of thirst—

grabbing, sucking, *feasting*, memorizing every inch as if I might disappear. He claims my nipples with his mouth and tugs on the piercings hard with his teeth. Fuck me, the pain is glorious. Mind-numbing.

"Fuck, you're unholy," he rumbles into my chest, his stubble like sandpaper against my skin. "Goddamn best pair of tits I've ever gotten my hands on."

"I can't imagine you've gotten your hands on many," I say with a smirk, and he looks up at me with an open-mouthed smile.

"You'd be surprised how many women I've fucked into insanity."

I pull him into another ravenous kiss, biting his lip hard enough to draw blood. Dark ichor drips onto his chin, and the taste of it sets my entire body on fire. It's somewhere between an acid trip and a rave, chaos magic flooding my system. Radiant. Electrifying.

I want to get lost in it.

"Make me bleed," I moan into our kiss, and he lets out one of those core-twisting chuckles again.

"Where?" His hand slides from my breasts to my torso, dragging his dull, human-glamoured nails until pink lines form in the pale skin. His fingers land between my legs, right over the coarse material of my dark jeans. "Here?"

"Anywhere." Instinctively, I grind into his palm, desperate for friction, desperate to feel pleasure and pain and mentally go anywhere but here.

Finally, he slips his hand into my jeans and between my legs.

And bites down on my lip. Hard.

His blood and mine mix on my tongue—dark and slick, iron-sweet and warm. His, demonic. Mine, ancient and wicked. Nails continue to drag down my back, and a cold rush floods through me as the fresh scratches erupt across my skin. A delicious, almost pathetic whine escapes me, and he devours it with his kiss.

Mayhem's fingers move inside me with perfect rhythm—slow, quick, quick, slow—like a perfect foxtrot. Every digit stretches me in the most delicious, almost painful way, and I drink up the ache with every breath.

The Underling is all-consuming. He towers over me, pulling away from our kiss to press his forehead to mine, all the while drawing me closer. Deeper. When his teeth find my shoulder, I suck in a sharp breath and brace myself for the next bite.

"I could make it hurt so much better," he groans against me, voice so hungry and desperate, it sounds like he's begging as he laps at the blood. "Let me use my *real* teeth. I could make you bleed so beautifully, baby. We'd put every Rorschach test to shame."

His words sink into me like hooks—a fucking Chaos demon wielding psychology terms like filthy promises, like some sort of deranged foreplay. It shouldn't be this tempting.

And yet, here I am, considering it.

But even the Devil's Second has limits.

"You're a sick fuck, Mayhem," I moan as he pushes another finger inside me.

And there's another deep, patronizing, *delicious* laugh. "Your crazy matches my crazy, Winters."

Grabbing his face and digging my nails into those devastatingly beautiful cheekbones, I pull him in for another kiss. His fingers move faster as our tongues dance wildly, and I've finally reached my limit with this particular foreplay.

"Knees. Now," I demand, digging my fingers into his hair and pull him away.

"Aw, aren't you cute?" he sing-songs a little too confidently. "Giving me orders."

"Fuck you," I growl, digging my nails into his scalp. "I'm above you, remember? You work for me." I push him down.

His knees buckle, but he remains upright, fingers still lodged deep inside me. "Tell me what you want, then, *kitten*." The word drops off his tongue in a moan, and I want to slap him across his beautiful face. "*Exactly* what you want."

"I told you." I shove him again, and, finally, he falls to his knees. "I think you can figure the rest out for yourself."

"Mmm." He withdraws his hand and licks his fingers, savoring the taste of me. "You love a man on his knees, don't you? Worshipping you."

"I also love a man with his mouth full of my cunt."

"Is *that* what you want?" He slowly unbuttons my jeans, inching them and my thong off my hips. He plants small, featherlight kisses on my thighs. "My mouth full of your cunt? Your come dripping down my chin?"

His eyes pin me in place. I hate that I want him to keep talking, hate that every word makes my pulse quicken. Grabbing another fistful of his dark hair, I shove his open, eager mouth between my legs.

And the demon begins to feast.

My own kaleidoscope explodes behind my eyelids. His tongue is sinful and chaotic, and those hungry moans claw from his throat, vibrating against my clit. I can't move—can't *breathe*. I can only surrender to the way he ravishes me.

I'm paralyzed by the pleasure, consumed by the ache.

And when he sinks his teeth into my thigh, I nearly sob.

"Was that necessary?" The words come out breathless, broken by moans. The pain sears white-hot where his teeth broke skin, heightened by the arousal pooling in my core. Every nerve ending screams as blood rushes to the wound.

His lips ghost along the bite mark. "You wanted me to make you bleed."

"I do," I groan as crimson trickles down my thigh.

"Then bleed for me."

There's something disconcerting about his human eyes. Somehow, they're far worse than his demonic ones. The kaleidoscope would mesmerize while the void would consume; these cold, dark heterochromatic eyes dissect. They strip away every defense, every lie, every buried secret until there's nothing left but my raw, exposed soul.

Everything about him devours, and after the year I've had…I could use a little mayhem of my own.

Time—or whatever semblance of time exists down here—suddenly stops.

The eerie energy misting around the 13 arches freezes mid-swirl. Cold tendrils wrap around my throat like ice, suffocating me as I look down to see my warm, ancient blood dripping into the waiting maw of the satanic ram.

That's when I feel Him.

He's everywhere and nowhere at once, practically stealing the air from my lungs. Panic coils in my stomach, twisting with the arousal still pooling there.

He can't be here. Not now. Not like this.

A large hand wraps gently around my throat, a surprisingly tender pressure against my skin. His imposing form presses against my back while another hand sweeps the hair from my neck. A deep purr rumbles from His chest as His lips ghost along my ear.

"Hello, Toby."

The Devil trails His hand from my neck down my sternum, lingering around the swell of my breasts. My breath hitches as I peer up at Him, taking in His beautiful features. "Boss, I'm a little busy—"

"I can see that." His chuckle vibrates throughout my entire body. "He doesn't mind—do you, Mayhem?"

The demon between my legs grins so wide, I almost forget he's wearing a glamour. The hunger in his eyes is electric, mirroring his kaleidoscope gaze, all while the knowing darkness could rival the void itself. He's completely unbothered by Lucifer's presence—if anything, it seems to fuel him. He continues his relentless task, coaxing me closer to orgasm, devouring every drop of me like I'm salvation itself.

Mayhem understands the dynamic completely. The rules. His place. This is his boss's boss, after all—the one who holds all the cards. The Underling is nothing but a pawn in this infernal game. A gift wrapped in chaos. A consolation prize to keep the rebellious, unpredictable Devil's Second on her leash.

Lucifer's gifts always come with chains, but that's tomorrow's problem. Tonight, in Hell's darkest circle, I'm going to let these dangerous, gorgeous things devour me.

I've fucking earned it.

I tilt my head back as the Devil claims my mouth. His kiss is a battle for dominance, and I'm losing—drowning in it, craving the moment He swallows me completely. The dark urge to defy Him tempts me. I long to push His buttons the way He pushes mine, to test the limits of His patience with my petulance. But when His grip on my neck tightens, I know He can feel that urge radiating off me. My eyes flutter shut as we kiss, His fingers dragging along the left side of my body until they find my nipple. Seconds later, another hand—Mayhem's—finds my right. Each touch is so different: one dominant and controlled, the other chaotic and hungry. My hands settle over theirs, savoring the worship of two dark beings giving my body exactly what it deserves.

My gaze drags languidly to the Underling still knelt between my legs, driving circles into my clit while his fingers pump in and out of me in a perfect rhythm. But Lucifer's hard fingers tighten around my neck.

"Don't look at him," the Devil commands in my ear. "Look at me. Only me." I swallow hard against His grasp, a single tear falling down my cheek as my eyes meet His. His are the coldest, most haunting shade of ice blue I've ever seen, drinking in the sight of me helpless in His hands. "In the presence of your King, I am the only thing that exists. Your eyes, your body, the very air in your lungs…it all belongs to me. Isn't that right, my disastrous little witch?"

I struggle to nod against His grip, my hips writhing relentlessly against Mayhem's tongue. Lucifer's fingers part my lips from behind, dragging the demon's saliva and my juices up the soft apex of my backside.

"Such an exquisite, rotten thing, isn't she, Mayhem?"

The Underling chuckles beneath me, sending delicious vibrations through my core.

"Don't you dare come on his tongue, October," Lucifer growls into my ear. "When you come, it'll be for me. Just for me."

"Then fuck me," I groan hungrily. "Fuck me, and make me come."

The King of Demons breathes out a chuckle so dangerous, so utterly devoid of warmth, that ice-cold dread locks my lungs. "I think she's had enough, Mayhem."

The fuck I have. I open my mouth to protest, but I'm distracted as Mayhem trails a path of hot, open-mouthed kisses up my stomach, nipping at my skin with every other one. When he finally stands, his gaze locks with the Devil's. They don't speak—not aloud. Some silent exchange passes between them, shared only in their minds, and for once, I wish I could hear them.

The Underling nods knowingly and steps aside, leaving my master and me alone. But he isn't gone: I can feel the chaos rolling off him from across the platform. Forever prickling. Distinctive.

Lucifer's in front of me now, towering over me with His striking, muscular frame. Taking my head in His hands, He kisses me softly, tongue slithering into my mouth to explore every inch, to taste my wickedness. He slowly guides us to the floor, inching the jeans and shoes off me completely until I'm laid bare. I'm in His lap in seconds, straddling His body, running my hands up and down His bare chest. A thick, black denim jacket hangs open, unbuttoned, framing the expanse of unholy skin beneath my palms. I reach into His leather pants, pulling out His throbbing length, and slowly, *finally*, lower myself onto it.

That unforgettable, magnificent cock.

The Devil and I have fucked many, *many* times. It's always been an act of power—a reminder of who owns whom, who surrenders to what. We've done it in stolen bodies, in fevered dreams, in the spaces between missions when we couldn't wait another second, but we've never had this. *His* territory. *His* time. No rush, no interruption, nothing but Him and me and the weight of what we are to each other.

I want to savor every fucking second.

"You move so beautifully," Lucifer groans as I circle my hips above Him, taking every inch of His cock, relishing the girth, the length. "I'd love to see how you'd writhe for one more."

His words stir something in me. Confusion. Discomfort. Curiosity. Maybe even anticipation. I meet those haunting eyes and tilt my head in question.

When I hear Mayhem's chuckle echo behind me, I finally understand.

The glamoured demon appears in my peripheral, clothes removed and hand fisting his cock as he watches me take the Devil. I try not to look at him—try to obey my master's command, to keep my eyes on Him and Him alone.

So, I rely on my other senses.

I scent him as he draws nearer, that peculiar mixture of something burnt and sweet all at once burning my nostrils, scents that should never mix but somehow do. His feet, now bare, pad quietly against ancient stone. Finally, I hear him settle behind me, and the familiar sensation of his touch returns.

One hand on my waist…and the other sliding gently between my rear cheeks.

He chuckles when I shiver from the contact. Something cold coats his fingers, a gel-like substance that he circles around my entrance, pushing against it delicately. Mayhem's finger enters me slowly, a perfect sensation added to the Devil's rigid, impossibly large cock nestled inside me.

His breath is hot and heavy against my shoulder as he licks the supple skin where he bit me. His other fingers dig into my hips as I reach behind to stroke his ridiculously hard cock, also coated in that cold substance. My ass pushes back to meet his abdomen, silently begging for what he has to offer. A breathy moan echoes throughout the platform when he withdraws his finger, and I guide him to my back entrance, meeting the pressure of him as he delicately pushes in.

The pain is fucking glorious, searing, white-hot, and enough to make me see stars. He's long—*so* long—and I take him inch by inch as he thrusts into my ass.

The tears flow heavier now as they fill me together, stretching my depths. Not from pain. Not from anguish.

From relief. From satisfaction. From pure and utter bliss.

Finally, I forget.

The impossible missions. Unbreakable curses. Power struggles, demonic politics. My horrible, impulsive decisions. A thousand years of mistakes.

Right here, right now, all that matters is pleasure and pain.

"That's it," Lucifer growls again. "Fuck yourself on us. Take what you need."

The King and the demon move in and out of me in perfect rhythm—so perfect, I wonder if they're communicating telepathically, coordinating each thrust with perfect precision. My cunt throbs around Lucifer's cock as I grind wildly against Him, my knees growing raw from the stone floor beneath me. I plant my hands firmly on His chest, holding myself up as they use me for their own pleasure. Lucifer marvels as his hands run from my hips up my sides. Sitting up, I allow my back to press against Mayhem's chest.

"Come for Him, kitten," he whispers into my ear,

nails scratching into my hips to draw blood again. "Light the fucking match." He drives deeper into me, his hips slapping against my ass in filthy, obscene ways. I'm reduced to nothing but guttural, feral moans as I ride the high of their dominance, desperate for the release that's been building since the minute Mayhem kissed me.

When the Devil reaches to squeeze my throat again, I finally do.

I come in a blaze of fire.

Literally.

My fire magic ignites, causing bursts of flames to erupt between each of the 13 arches circling the platform. The souls of the dead wail beneath us in the Pit, flocking to the flames like moths. Above us, a swarm of spirits twists and writhes, and my heart pounds in my throat as my orgasm rushes through me. For a moment—a fleeting moment—I wonder how many of those souls I sent here. How many of those lost, wayward souls were never claimed by a Prime or their realm. How they wander for eternity with no salvation in the fieriest depths of Hell.

But I don't care. I fucking hate them all. The living. The dead. Their lives were nothing but currency.

Lucifer's lips crash to mine again, sucking me in as my fire flickers against our bodies.

"So beautiful," He whispers against my lips, "to watch you come undone. To watch the most powerful witch in Hell become putty in our hands. Such a beauti-ful, *perfect* thing."

His praise sends warmth flooding through me. He and Mayhem withdraw from me simultaneously, and the whine that escapes my chest is downright pathetic. The emptiness returns, and while I long for more—long to be used and fucked within an inch of my life—I remember there's one last bit of satisfaction I haven't collected.

I find the strength to stand, even while my aching joints thrum with pleasure and pain. My fire dissipates around me, leaving us in darkness, save for the ambient light of the 13 portals. The spirits return to the Pit of the Lost beneath the suspended platform, right where they belong—far away from me. I dress quickly, pulling my tight dark jeans over my sticky, sweaty, bloodied skin and my tank top over my chest. My eyes land on that fucking stupid gate swarming with insects. Right at the base of the arch is my little scorpion—Declan Lovejoy.

I smirk at my familiar, knowing he can scent every dirty, grimy inch of me—of *them*, knowing he heard every single word, every moan, every plea. I crouch to his level.

"Hope you enjoyed the show," I whisper as I pick up the scorpion in its frozen state. His thoughts are still silent, but I can feel his fury, his anguish, feel the torment that will forever plague him.

Venom drips from my lips as I cast the spell that turns him back into jewelry.

I've had a thousand years to perfect the art of fucking up. A thousand years, and I made twice as many mistakes. Binding my ex-lover as my familiar for the rest of my immortal life wasn't my brightest idea. It was impulsive, vindictive, and spectacularly diabolical. Classic October Winters.

And I wouldn't have it any other way.

Lucifer awaits me at the center of the platform, right above the summoning maw. Behind me, Mayhem's still glamoured, preoccupied with dressing himself—buckling his belt and harness, lacing his boots. I shrug my leather jacket over my shoulder and meet the Devil's gaze head-on.

"Satisfied?" His small smirk sends a shiver down my spine.

"I am now." I slip the ring on my finger and step closer to Him. "We need to talk."

The King of Demons regards me with a raised eyebrow. When He stays silent, I continue.

"I didn't need an escort to guide me through the Nightmare and Fear Realm, Lucifer." I use His real name to signal how serious this is. "Even if I went in alone, the outcome would have been the same. So why did you assign Mayhem to me?"

The Devil stares down at me, and suddenly, I feel incredibly small. "Your soul has been lost for quite some time, my firestarter. You needed someone to remind you who you are—and how dangerous you can be." I resist the urge to roll my eyes at the melodrama. "You needed to be reminded that, despite everything, you're not alone."

"I *am* alone," I mutter under my breath, and I practically cringe at how pathetic I sound.

"You'll always have me." His clawed thumb caresses right under my Marked eye. "Even with your laundry list of debts to pay for your betrayals…I'll always need you by my side."

"Don't do that," I murmur, avoiding His gaze. "The whole soft and caring act. It doesn't suit you."

A deep chuckle rumbles through His chest, but it's not amusement. It's dark, predatory—a sound that reminds me exactly who I'm dealing with.

"You failed your mission."

Heat crawls up my neck and burns my cheeks. "Not failed. Derailed. I know what I need to break the curse. I just…need permission back Upstairs."

"Granted," He says without hesitation. "But take Mayhem with you."

"I don't need—"

"Take. Mayhem. With. You." Each word drops like a stone. "He will keep you focused…and satisfy whatever dark appetites your body craves."

His voice softens, which somehow makes it more terrifying. "I told you, my rotten darling: he's my gift to you. Another belated birthday present, if you will." He steps closer until His presence swallows me whole. "You may have him to play with, and he will play with you—he'll worship you, satisfy you, give you whatever you ask. But he will never burn the world for you. Not like I would. So, at the end of every night, when the embers cease and the ashes settle, you'll remember who plays with you the hardest. You belong to me, October Winters. Your heart made that choice long ago."

That choice.

The truth never tasted so sweet and poisonous all at once.

My gaze flits to the obsidian ring on my finger—the reminder of what happens to those who try to change me. Forever trapped in a prison of his own making, of my design, Lovejoy taught me I will never compromise. Not for anyone.

I'm not someone to be redeemed. To be saved. To be fixed.

The Devil over my shoulder is proof of that. The demon between my legs was the prize.

But the true prize is not the acceptance of others.

It's the intoxicating freedom of accepting myself.

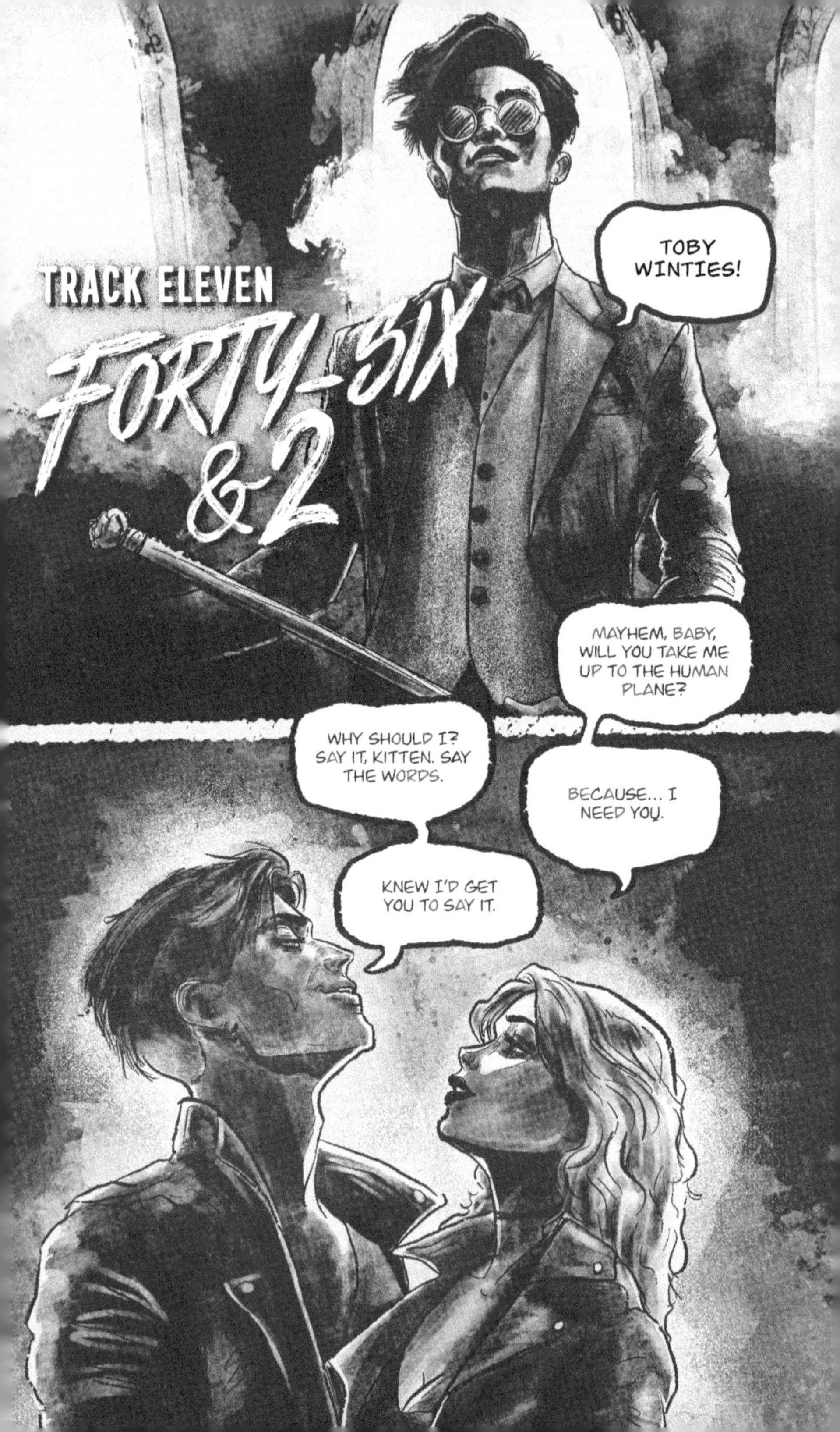

TRACK ELEVEN
FORTY-SIX & 2

TRACK ELEVEN

FORTY-SIX & 2

Time starts to move again once the Devil vanishes into the shadows. Eerie mist swirls around the arches, colors begin to flicker and pulse, and, somewhere beyond the platform, the faint racket of blabbering demons resumes.

I barely have a second to catch Mayhem's eye before the platform trembles violently beneath our feet. I brace myself against the nearest arch—thankfully not crawling with insects—as crimson smoke explodes across the stone in a shimmering cloud. The air fills with that sickeningly sweet scent of overripe fruit mixed with something darker, something dripping in sin.

And then, a demon materializes.

No, not a demon—a Prime. Dressed to kill in his glittery, gaudy best, red sunglasses perched perfectly on his nose, and a crystal-tipped cane catching the Hellish light.

I wish I could wipe the grin off his stupid face.

"Toby Winties!"

"Your timing is fucking impeccable as always," I groan as the Demon of Debauchery hops off the satanic ram's head symbol and saunters toward me with theatrical flair.

"Pure coincidence this time, darling." Cherry waves his hand dismissively. "Simply caught me between realms."

I finally get a good look at him—disheveled hair, wrinkled suit, tie askew. This is nothing like the immaculate Cherry I know. "The fuck happened to you?"

"I could ask you the same," he replies, gesturing toward my face, taking in the mismatched irises and black veins spiderwebbing just below my left eye and cheekbone. "Halloween was weeks ago, love. Bit late for the special effects makeup, don't you think?"

"It's a Mark," I blurt out too quickly. "The Mark of Nightmares and Fear."

Cherry sucks in a sharp breath and shakes his head. "Still haven't kissed and made up with the twins, have you? Pity." He waves his fingers dismissively. "Allow me to take care of that for you."

With a quick flourish and muttered Hellspeak, Cherry weaves his magic. Mayhem's eyebrows shoot up as he steps closer, studying my face. "The fuck. He glamoured your eye back to normal."

"Goodness, you're a fine specimen, aren't you?" Cherry purrs, looking Mayhem up and down. "And who in the 13 realms might you be?"

"Mayhem, First of Chaos."

"*Chaos*?" Cherry's voice pitches higher, almost scandalized. "That tubby little bastard sired *you*? You're far too gorgeous to be one of his. A First, no less."

Mayhem shoots him a predatory grin. "I'm much prettier in my demon form."

"Somehow, I doubt that," Cherry mutters.

He reaches into his breast pocket and produces a handheld mirror. I fumble for it with shaking hands, desperate to see my own reflection. My normal hazel stares back at me, and something in my chest loosens… briefly. Then, I notice my hair. It's longer, past my shoulders—time I don't remember losing. How fucking long have I been down here?

"How long will this last, Cherry?"

"Indefinitely, unless you cast something strong enough to break it. But it's just a glamour, darling—a Mark is still a Mark, even with the best concealer."

"Too bad." Mayhem shrugs, his gaze lingering on my face. "I kinda liked it on ya."

Cherry's eyes light up with delight, catching the ever-so-slight blush creeping up my cheeks. "Oh. *Oh.*

This is delicious." He claps his hands together. "Winties, darling, you've got yourself a new fuck toy? You could have had the pick of my litter. Debauchery Underlings are *far* more satisfying than a Chaos demon. I know how much you love that crimson cupcake of mine in Hollywood—"

"How is Reagan anyway?" I cut him off before he can elaborate.

"She's got her hands full with a little"—Cherry waves his hand vaguely—"charge of mine."

I raise an eyebrow. "Charge?"

"Best not bore you with the details." Cherry glides over to one of the arches—naturally, the most ornate one.

Its gate ripples like liquid mercury while swirls of red, gold, and black dance around it in hypnotic, tantalizing patterns. I catch a glimpse of the engraving above, and I'm not surprised the prettiest gate belongs to him. He catches his reflection in the mirror-like surface and clicks his tongue in disgust at his disheveled state. He waves his hand like some sort of elaborate magician. Instantly, he's transformed into a new sparkling ensemble, complete with a bow tie so gaudy, it could blind someone.

"Ah, much better. Right then, what's all this bother with you and the twins? Perhaps I could lend a hand."

His offer sounds generous, but I don't trust it as far

as I can throw him. Like his Father, Cherry's gifts always come with strings attached. I'm still waiting for the other shoe to drop from our last little arrangement—his so-called "birthday present."

Still, I spill the story.

He listens intently, nodding dramatically, demonic eyes practically glittering behind his red-tinted shades. I conveniently leave out the finer details—Eve, Lovejoy, the parts that would give him far too much leverage over me. All he needs to know is that my mission is to break the banishment curse, and the only way to do that is to hand over a pure Nephilim soul for them to consume.

No corruption. No darkness. The purest, most Divine soul I could find.

And I'm fresh out of those.

My stomach clenches. *You're not totally fresh out,* a voice in my head whispers. *You still have hers.* But despite every logical, practical fiber in my being screaming that it's the perfect solution, it isn't. Not by a long shot.

Eve's soul is not pure. How could it be? Part of it was forged from my own wickedness, tainted by the corruption in her father's heart—a Nephilim who broke every sacred rule to be with an evil witch.

No. Eve's soul is mine and mine alone, and I'll be damned if I hand it over to some Prime who doesn't deserve it.

Mayhem is at my side in an instant, his hand wrapping around my elbow and pulling me toward him. The sensation of his skin against mine is welcome now—especially after the intimacy we shared, even knowing everything between us has shifted. I turn to look at him, and there's something new in his eyes, a protective darkness that wasn't there before.

I'll deal with the emotional garbage of it all later.

"We should head topside," Mayhem murmurs, his voice low and firm. "We've got a job to do."

"*I've* got a job to do," I murmur back. "I don't care what Lucifer said. This is my problem, and I need to get out of it."

"A lover's quarrel, how sweet. It'll make for glorious makeup sex later, I'm sure." Cherry regards Mayhem curiously for a moment, tilting his head to the side. "I imagine the stamina on a Chaos demon is outrageous. I wouldn't mind watching—for my own curiosity, of course."

"You're a little late for that," I snap, throwing my jacket on. "Alright, Demon of Semen, I'd hate to blow my load too early—"

"Don't worry, darling. It happens to the best of us." He shoots me a wink.

"—but I've gotta bounce. Need to hunt down a Nephilim."

Cherry's perfectly manicured brows shoot up. "Fresh out of those, are you?"

"My last one found out exactly what happens when you mess with the Devil's Second. Let's just say he won't be making that mistake again." I twist the ring around my finger with a sly smile.

"But there was another, wasn't there?" Cherry hums, tapping his finger against his pursed lips. "The apprentice."

Bingo. The little weasel who slipped through my fingers, the one whose name is too fucking insignificant to remember… Jamantha…Jordypoo…whatever the Hell it was.

Him.

He was my plan all along.

Cherry and I exchange twin grins, but before either of us can speak, his entire body erupts in violent shivers. "Well, well, it appears one of my Underlings is summoning me." His lips twist into a sly, predatory smile. "You were on your way up anyway. Why don't you join me, Winties?"

"Why the fuck would I do that?"

"Because I possess something you need." His finger trails just above the sharp edge of his cheekbone, tapping beneath his eye—referring to my Mark. Color me intrigued. I meet his gaze with knitted brows, and he adds, "Something that will break that pesky curse."

The pieces continue to click, but I'm not easily convinced. "You mean to tell me you have a Nephilim just lying around somewhere to pawn off on me?"

"Let's say I do," he muses.

"Bullshit," I spit. "I think I'd know if a Prime possessed a Nephilim soul."

His spine-tingling laugh echoes throughout the platform. "Just like you knew when we were collecting them before? Before you conveniently helped that hunter bring them back?"

My mind flashes back to the night Lovejoy and I infiltrated that demonic lounge, discovering the ritual of banishment and hatching our own brilliant plan to recover the missing Nephilim. The same plan that landed me in this mess.

Cherry steps closer. "You want nothing to do with us demons, remember, Toby? You've spent the better part of your immortal existence ignoring and berating us." He feigns offense, jutting out his lower lip with that condescending voice. "Not to mention your year-long sabbatical." He clicks his tongue three times, and if he doesn't watch it, I'll rip it out before he can do it again. "For all you know, I have an entire strip club of them waiting to be devoured."

Now *that* would be a sight. I almost believe him, but my narrowed eyes and clenched jaw show I'm not easily convinced.

"What do you want in exchange?" I don't bother softening my tone. "I already owe you."

He waves his hand with another sickening giggle. "I told you, love, that was a birthday present."

"Getting real tired of all these fucking birthday presents I never asked for." I lean against the Debauchery arch and fold my arms, crossing my ankles. "What do you want for the Nephilim?"

Cherry shivers again, and I realize he still has a summons to return. My heart rate spikes—I cannot let him leave without an answer.

"Meet me at Bad Decisions at 9:00 a.m. Come alone." He winks at Mayhem. "And don't be late."

In seconds, the Demon of Debauchery vanishes just as quickly as the Devil did. I drag my hands down my face, streaking black makeup down my cheeks, and I let out a groan so loud and frustrated, it bounces off every arch in this godforsaken place.

Finally, Mayhem and I are alone.

He's lingering by his own arch now, pretending to be preoccupied with the bees swarming the portal. He catches one with his bare hands, crushes it, and pops it in his mouth without breaking eye contact.

"Please tell me you have a way up." I search through my jacket pockets for my grimoire, flipping through pages of my own scribbled, messy handwriting—eons of spells—searching for the Hellspeak incantations to get us out of here. "Mayhem?" I ask when he ignores me.

His head snaps up, eyes innocent but unfazed. "Now you want my help?"

"Oh, come on," I groan. "You heard Lucifer."

"I heard him loud and clear. But you, babe, are giving me mixed signals. I don't do well with mixed signals—I get enough of those up here." He twirls his fingers near his temple. "I'm going to need to hear you say it. Pretend I'm stupid."

I narrow my eyes. "I don't need to pretend."

"Ouch, baby. That how you're gonna talk to your only way out of Hell?"

With another loud, exasperated sigh, I approach him, practically dragging my feet across the ancient stone. When I reach him, I step dangerously close, toying with the rough leather of his belt, slipping my finger under the hem of his neatly tucked fishnet mesh shirt. I flash him the most innocent eyes I can muster and drop my voice to a soft, seductive whisper.

"Mayhem, *baby*," I start, leaning in so close, my nose practically nuzzles his neck. Fuck, he smells good—how can a Chaos demon smell so intoxicating? "Will you take me up to the human plane?"

He chuckles, twisting one gloved finger in my now-longer, disheveled blonde hair. "Why should I?"

"Because..." I trail off, my fingers sliding lower to the growing evidence of his interest. Hah—Chaos stamina. Could give Cherry's incubi a run for their money.

"Say it, kitten. Say the words."

I could punch him if his human form wasn't so devastatingly attractive. Everything from that widow's peak to his mismatched blue-green and dark brown eyes, the sharp curve of his lips, and those cheekbones that could cut glass…

Ugh. Fine.

"I need you," I whisper against his throat, pressing my body flush against him.

He pulls back slightly, staring down at me with half-lidded, darkening eyes. "Knew I'd get you to say it."

I swat his chest playfully, backing away with a grin. "Don't get used to it."

He rubs his hands together, approaching the maw in the center of the room. "Where we headed?"

"Hollywood. You ever been?"

"Fuckin' hate that place. But the '90s sure were one Hell of a time." He flashes me that toothy grin as he crouches beside the ram's head and pricks his finger on one of the fangs. Black ichor seeps into the stone mouth.

Within seconds, the ram's eyes and mouth ignite with Hellish red light. Mayhem takes my hand and mutters the incantation under his breath.

Before I know it, we're back in the City of Angels.

The familiar smog hits my lungs, and for the first time, I'm grateful to inhale the fumes. Cars rush past below us, the ambient noise of the city like music to my ears.

We're standing atop Mount Hollywood, right below

the gargantuan letter *H* of the Hollywood sign. Hell's portal seals shut behind us. The sun barely peeks over Downtown LA's skyline, painting the entire city breathtaking hues of pink and orange.

It's morning. Cold as Hell too, and the irony doesn't escape me.

Judging by the few orange-leafed trees scattered among the evergreens and the sharp bite in the air, it's definitely the start of winter. End of November, probably. As the familiar chaos of Hollywood sprawls before me, I can't shake the feeling that darker times lie ahead. The Mark burns behind my glamoured eye—a constant reminder that the twins will always be watching.

I glance at Mayhem beside me, still holding my hand, still wearing that dangerous grin, and I realize I'm not the same witch who descended into the Underworld.

Lucifer was right—it was never about how long the mission would take. It was about whether I'd survive it.

The jury's still out on that one.

We descend into the city in my Camaro, tires burning rubber against asphalt. We sit in comfortable silence, my token death metal blasting through the damaged speakers, and despite the nerves clawing at me, I manage to nod my head to the rhythm. Music has always been my salvation, always spoken to whatever's left of my soul.

"So…" Mayhem breaks the silence, glancing at me

sideways, mischief dripping from his tone. "We gonna talk about what happened down there?"

I keep my eyes on the road ahead, gripping the steering wheel tighter. "We already talked about it. Nothing more to say—just gotta go in, get that Nephilim, and head back Downstairs. Put this whole thing behind us so those bastards can get off my ass and go back to torturing humans."

"No. Not that." His insufferable smirk sends a thousand ants crawling up my spine. "The double-team pound sesh with my gramps."

My stomach lurches. "That's…that's not even accurate, dude. He isn't your grandpa."

"If you *really* break it down—"

"Nope." I cut him off sharply. "Not your grandpa. You're a demonic construct born from another demonic construct. The Devil has no blood relations, no family tree, just weird demon frat boy mentality magic shit." I grind my molars at the thought. "Like I said, there's nothing more to talk about. And you can wipe that shit-eating grin off your face."

"Why should I? I fucked the Devil's Second. How many demons can say that? You were delightful, by the way." His grin widens. "Bangin' bod, killer tits, *delicious* pussy—and that thing you did at the end? Stellar, babe." He kisses his fingertips, like a chef appreciating fine cuisine. "So, what did you like about me?"

My eyes couldn't possibly roll harder. "The part where you stopped talking."

"Harsh but fair." He chuckles. "My mouth was busy doing other things."

I slam the brakes, lurching us both forward with a violent jolt. The Bad Decisions neon sign hangs dark and lifeless as I study the entrance, and suddenly, dread washes over me like ice water. The radio said today was November 29—fresh off Thanksgiving, heading into the holidays. That's almost a month since I've breathed mortal-realm air. One month since I last saw that beautiful red-haired succubus. One month since…

I twist the ring on my finger, forcing myself to focus on the task at hand: reuniting with the only woman I consider a friend. And Cherry—the only Prime who's publicly, willingly allied himself with me despite the shitstorm brewing in the Underworld, much to his brothers' disdain.

Any trace of what I did during those six days leading up to Halloween has vanished. Clear skies, bright sun, locals and tourists flooding Hollywood's streets like nothing ever happened—this city thrives on lies and cover-ups. I'm glad to see some things never change.

With a wave of my hand, the Camaro's engine dies. I'm parked in my usual spot at The Starlight motel's nearly empty lot, steeling myself for what's coming. Get in, get out. I can't imagine how Cherry snagged a

Nephilim or how he's hiding them at Bad Decisions, but the bastard's always been full of surprises.

I push the thought away. I don't give a shit about the how or why.

I just need that fucking Nephilim, whoever they are.

"Hey, wait—" Mayhem catches my wrist before I exit the car. I turn to face him, this Chaos demon wearing human skin, those dark graphite eyes melting me from the inside. He's devastating to look at, and the longer I stare, the more I want him to devour me again. But there's something gentle in his gaze now, something I couldn't see in his demonic form.

He takes my hand, and I find myself tracing the maze of tattoos covering his knuckles and snaking up his forearms like living art.

"I know you don't need my approval, validation, or worship." His voice is velvet soft, achingly tender. "But I'd like to give 'em to you anyway."

"Why? You owe me nothing." The words tumble out before I can stop them, but the truth sits heavy in my chest—I know why. I know he was hand-picked by the Devil to remind me of my power, to keep me tethered. Still, I want to hear him say it.

"You never ask for mercy in the face of your enemies, even when faced with your greatest fears. That's strength. That's resilience. Something to be proud of." His grip tightens slightly. "I won't pretend to understand what happened down there. The beef with the twins, your familiar—your...kid." He winces at the word, and my heart tightens. "But whatever you did a year ago, whatever earned you that six-day ultimatum with the Big Guy, you did it because you thought it was necessary. And that's good enough for me."

It's not what I expected, and the sentiment worms its way into my cold heart, threatening to melt it from the inside. So, I deflect with brutal honesty.

"Lucifer gifted you to me. You're a toy—a stress reliever. Let's not pretend you actually like me."

"Oh, but I fucking do. And I hate dead people too." He chuckles at his unintentional rhyme. "You might think this is all for show because Big Daddy Downstairs called in a favor with my boss, but I wasn't kidding when I said I've been dying to meet you. I'd have found a way with or without His help." Mayhem's subtle smirk grows into a grin that rivals his demonic form. "Don't look so surprised, kitten. Of the Thirteen, the Chaos Broodline fucking adores you the most. You're just as batshit as we are."

"Jesus fucking Christ," I mutter under my breath. "Of all the Primes."

"Don't knock it. When shit hits the fan, you'll want Chaos on your side—not against ya."

His words sink in, and I hate that he's right. Cherry's alliance can only protect me so much. I need an offensive Prime in my corner. All I can hope for is that Cherry delivers on his "gift," so I can be done with this cluster-fuck and move on with the rest of my immortal life.

If only it were that simple.

I grip the steering wheel, feeling the old leather crack beneath my fingertips. Everything is still raw inside, but Mayhem's right—I'm batshit crazy. I'll never beg for mercy, and I'll never apologize for the choices I've made.

"Your job's done," I say, grabbing my purse and slinging it over my shoulder. "Time to go back to the icky depths you crawled out of."

Mayhem's head hits the back of the headrest, dimples highlighting his helpless yet mischievous smile. "You know, it's been a little too hot down there lately. I could use the fresh air." His gaze meets mine. "I'm not going anywhere. You're stuck with me, baby. Now, get outta here. You've got a 9:00 a.m. you don't wanna miss. I'll keep the car warm."

The irony is fucking perfect—the only stable thing in my cursed existence is a literal agent of chaos. Go figure. I flash him a grin. "You're insane, you know that?"

He pats his chest and winks with what would usually be his kaleidoscope eye. "That's why they call me Mayhem."

I lean over to brush a chaste kiss against his cheek, but his fingers catch the back of my neck, pulling my lips to his in something fierce and all-consuming. He holds us there—two wicked creatures basking in each other's darkness, devouring a passion that could burn cities to ash. In his kiss, I taste potential. In his kiss, I taste chaos.

When I finally pull away, breathless, he looks into my eyes, and I swear he's drawing me into the same mania he's inflicted on countless others.

"Go," he says, voice rough with want.

And I do.

TRACK TWELVE
SUPER BEAST

LET'S JUST SAY
I TRADED MY
EARRING IN FOR
SOMETHING
MORE...SYMBOLIC.

TRACK TWELVE

SUPERBEAST

I LOVE MAKING AN ENTRANCE—ALMOST AS MUCH AS I LOVE making a dramatic exit.

It's probably because of that sick, twisted part of me that craves attention and worship, the little egomaniac I do fuck-all to keep buried. Why should I? Life's too short to stay humble and hidden in the shadows—I did that for too long, and all it got me was ultimatums, demonic brain-fucks, and a shitty ex-lover I'll get to torment for the rest of my life.

When life has no expiration date, you've got to get a little creative.

I should patent that shit.

I slam open the doors to Bad Decisions, morning sun casting a long shadow across aged linoleum and crusty carpet. And then, I see her. That brilliant, beautiful red-haired demoness—a sight for sore eyes if there ever was one. Her features twitch in disbelief, but the smile spreading across her face tells me everything I need to know: she missed the fuck out of her favorite witch.

"October fucking Winters."

It's good to be back.

But I absolutely did not expect the nightmare waiting for me.

I try to mask my absolute shock with one of my signature grins, leaning against the threshold as I take in Bad Decisions—the seedy strip club that served as my temporary refuge just a month ago. It looks the same, save for some dusting and shinier poles, but it isn't the club that has my heart plummeting into my stomach.

It's the abomination that takes center stage.

As I step closer, the horror becomes clearer. There's a figure bound to the main pole—a writhing, glowing monstrosity with lightning fractures spiderwebbing through its flesh, lines pulsing. It's somewhere between human and something else entirely. His eyes burn white-hot like headlights, and jagged bones erupt through his skull and spine. They form twisted, spine-like horns and skeletal wings that twitch with each labored breath. Where his skin hasn't split open, it's stretched taut and translucent, revealing the sickening glow of whatever's consuming him from the inside.

Jeremy Roache—that pathetic little toad who used to grovel at my ex-lover's feet, who foolishly swore to destroy me—is a demon.

And from the looks of his convulsing, tortured state, he's brand fucking new.

Well, fuck me sideways. There goes my leverage.

I catch Cherry's shaded eyes, teeth grinding behind a forced smile. He looks just as bewildered as I am, though unbearably smug about it. Was this his doing? Did he orchestrate some elaborate trap?

I smother the rising panic with what I do best: sadistic mockery.

"Well, well, well. If it isn't the little roach himself. Demonhood suits you, Jiggory."

"For the last time, you evil fucking bitch." Jeremy's growl reverberates along with the lights, flickering throughout the club. "My name is *Jeremy*."

A sickening giggle escapes me. "I wouldn't be announcing that all over town if I were you. Knowing the name of a demon comes with plenty of perks for me, but it absolutely *sucks* for you." Jeremy snarls at me, saliva continuing to drip from his lips. "Down, boy."

I don't even know where to fucking start.

A laundry list of questions floods my brain—how the fuck? Why the fuck? When the fuck?

When I left Hollywood, Jeremy was lost to me, exactly as he should be. I couldn't have cared less where he slithered off to. I'd hoped he would waste away mourning his losses or crawl back to his pathetic Order with his tail between his legs. But instead, he's here. In

Bad Decisions. Cowering at Reagan's feet like a broken pet, gazing up at her as if she's his salvation.

The longer I stare at this twisted tableau, the more the questions multiply.

My mind races a million miles an hour, the club suddenly suffocating with the four of us crammed inside. The Mark on my eye, so graciously glamoured by Cherry, burns like acid—a constant reminder that the twins are watching from below, that my mission is nowhere near finished.

In fact, I'm royally fucked.

In the span of seconds, my only bargaining chip has transformed into the very thing that could destroy everything. I'm back to square one, desperately hunting for a pure Nephilim soul to deliver to the twins. All while dodging a vengeful poltergeist hell-bent on my destruction and a handful of other Primes who will gleefully watch me crash and burn.

They can't see me falter. I need to appear detached.

Masking the panic forming in my chest, I find the bar, rummaging through the incubus bartender's stash before popping open an untainted beer bottle and taking a swig.

"Place looks less like shit than the last time I saw it." I take a seat on the bar top, crossing my legs and lighting a cigarette with a snap of my fingers. "You clean up recently?"

Reagan smirks. "Thought you were done with us

after torching the cemetery. What brings you back to our little slice of Hell?"

Fuck, it feels so long ago now. The six-day ultimatum, the tragic ending, the nightmares that followed. Time will never make sense down there. But the blonde locks now grown past my shoulder are evidence enough that I was there for far too long.

I take a long drag, letting smoke curl between us. "Came to have a little chat with Cherry, but it seems like this science experiment is worth a closer look." God, I'm barely holding it together, desperately trying to appear unfazed by this clusterfuck, but I'm seconds from losing my shit. Only sheer force of will keeps me from cracking. "How the fuck did you manage…whatever this is?"

"Marvelous, isn't it?" Cherry glides over, leaning in for his customary two-cheeked kiss. "A demon-Nephilim hybrid—first of its kind. And from my Brood-line, no less."

"You must be so proud." My voice is flat. "I can see it now: 'World's first Dephilim, straight from the infernal loins of the Demon of Debauchery.' Oh, how your brothers will cower at the thought of a super-beast who can fuck them to death—"

"Where's Declan's body?" Jeremy growls, cutting the Prime off. "Whatever you did, you had no right. He didn't deserve it!"

Oh, I have zero tolerance for this Batman & Robin bullshit. I simply tilt my head in mock admiration, placing a hand over my heart. "Aww, how cute—it has opinions. Looks like you finally grew not just one spine, but two." I gesture at the vertebrae-like horns jutting from his skull.

What follows is a twisted game laid out for me to dissect. This verbal volleyball of banter and revelations drags on for what feels like an eternity. I discover it wasn't Cherry who created this abomination, but my darling Reagan—a high-ranking succubus who managed to corrupt the incorruptible and backed Cherry into a corner.

She speaks with pride, with the confidence she's always possessed, but it feels…different now. Stronger. Brighter. She's absolutely *radiant*.

But I can read between the lines, past the carefully constructed façade. There's pain in her eyes. Guilt. And with every stolen glance at the angel-turned-demon, the devastating truth crystallizes.

Reagan fell in love with him. A demon fell in love with an angel. And then, she shattered his heart.

She's no better than me. We're just two sides of the same fucked-up coin.

I absolutely adore her for it.

But really, Reagan? *Him*? Ugh.

I watch her eviscerate Cherry's pride, standing tall and regal like the demonic goddess she is, demanding what she's owed from her Prime. I couldn't be more enchanted by her in this moment. My eyebrows climb toward my hairline as she reveals her trump card—how she accomplished what no other Underling could manage, and now, she demands her rightful seat at the apex of demonic hierarchy.

Not as an equal to Cherry's Sired.

But as the Debauchery Prime herself.

As Cherry crumbles into a mess of pathetic whimpering, though, I'm transfixed by the disaster that is Jeremy Roache.

His eyes never leave me. He watches me like a starved predator, ready to tear me apart. My mere presence is a taunt—a living reminder that evil triumphed and good failed spectacularly.

A small, quiet voice suddenly whispers in my head.

It's faint at first—a ghost of a murmur I think I'm imagining. But as the seconds tick by and the Debauchery Prime and her Underling continue their power struggle, the voice in my skull grows louder.

What have they done to him?

I freeze as reality slices through me. My eyes dart to my ring, panicked I might have accidentally awakened my scorpion and given him access to my thoughts.

But the ring remains just a ring. All asshole, no glow.

You never quit, do you, Lovejoy? How the fuck did you get in my head? I send him a mental snarl, still reeling from this impossible development.

He was pure. He was everything I failed to be. Lovejoy's

mental voice cracks with anguish. *And they destroyed him. You've all destroyed him.*

Cry me a river. I grow tired of this Shakespearean melodrama. I fold my arms over my chest, angling my ring away from the scene while trying to keep up with the conversation, tossing out witty barbs at Cherry's expense.

But Lovejoy's still there. Still in my head. Still seeing through my eyes, feeling every cruel thought that crosses my mind.

I work harder to push him down, to slam the mental door shut and lock him out.

Somewhere within it all, Cherry ceases his own theatrics, and his demeanor shifts to one of indifference.

"You don't want this job, love," he tells Reagan, desperately trying to break her of her demands. "It's all sex, drugs, and rock and roll—you'd grow tired of it."

"I wouldn't," I reply with a shrug. Lovejoy's anguish continues to fester in my mind, turning into something dangerously close to fury. But I need to keep up my own façade. They can't know what's going on in my mind.

That's when Reagan flashes me a conspiratorial grin. "Perhaps you and I should be the next Debauchery Primes then."

Well, that's a thought—one I have absolutely no interest in taking. Becoming a Prime only means more paperwork, more subordinates to manage, and less room for me to torture the innocent.

Though, if I had to be *any* Prime, the Debauchery Prime wouldn't be the worst.

Getting rid of Cherry would certainly solve a lot of my problems.

"Look at you. Two peas in a bloody pod," Cherry practically spits. "And to think, your paths would have never crossed all those years ago if not for me."

"All those years ago?"

My blood turns to ice. Where the fuck is Cherry going with this? I've never met Reagan before the ultimatum—she's just another succubus. One I've grown fond of, sure, but I'd remember someone as magnificent as her if our paths had crossed.

Wouldn't I?

"Oh, did I leave out that little detail? Silly me. I thought you knew."

Every instinct screams at me to start running. Before Cherry even has a chance to puff out his chest and drop another bombshell on us, my feet itch to flee. But his melodic, charming voice anchors me in place.

"Savannah's lovely in the summertime, isn't it, Toby? Before all this global warming nonsense. And the hurricanes were such an easy place to reap souls, with all the dead bodies lying around, especially at the dawn of a new decade. Why, it was almost serendipitous that you happened to be in town when one of my Sired and I were attending a funeral. You remember, don't you,

Winties? That behemoth of a mansion with Gothic interiors and lovely red accents?"

The memory surfaces like a body from deep water—vague, fleeting—but the rotary wheel of recollections spins in my head until it finally clicks into place.

Savannah, 1911. A funeral. An open casket harboring a debaucherous soul ripe for harvesting. I was behind on my quota for the month—fucking sue me. If Cherry and his raven-haired succubus hadn't thrown me that bone, I would've been on probation with the Devil himself.

Plus, it gave me an excuse to absolutely slay the mourners in my gorgeous black funeral dress.

Still, I shrug. Practiced indifference. Masterful nonchalance. "I've been around for a thousand years and reaped millions of souls. You think I remember every house I've visited or every soul I've collected?"

"Ah, but you remember this one, don't you? The little arrangement we made between reapings?"

"That was you?" Reagan asks, voice cracking. "The woman crying over my husband's casket? You took his soul?"

That's when the rest of the conversation fades to white noise. Cherry—ever the fucking cunt—spills his diabolical history to Reagan, who looks like we all took turns stabbing her in the back.

But that's when it hits me like a freight train.

Cherry never intended to deliver me a Nephilim. He

never intended to get played by Reagan either. He was cornered by two ruthless women and desperately clawed his power back.

He played us both.

Typical fucking Prime. How could I be so goddamn stupid?

I need to get out of here.

Reality is like the worst kind of infection—just when you think it's gone, it flares up and reminds you how fucked you really are.

Meanwhile, my ex-lover's deep, haunting voice continues to echo in my head.

You really do destroy everything you touch, don't you?

You should know. I twist the ring around my finger with deliberate cruelty.

Jeremy! Lovejoy's voice screams in my ears. He repeats the pest's name over and over, as if desperate to get his attention, as if the demon could *actually* hear him.

But that's when it hits me.

Debauchery demons can read minds.

And the last thing I need right now is for Lovejoy to break through to Jeremy and give him the strength he needs to destroy me.

I need to get the fuck out of here.

My mind becomes chaos incarnate, and I'm unable to silence the cacophony—Lovejoy's screams, Summer's wails, every soul I've ever reaped all shrieking in unison. It's enough to drive me over the edge.

Everything blurs together, suffocating me as fears I never knew existed writhe and claw within my chest, igniting the searing pain in my Marked eye.

I'm on my feet before conscious thought kicks in. I lunge for the door, but Reagan calls my name. I ignore her.

"Fuck!" I jerk my hand back from the burning door handle, shaking off the pain. Fire has never hurt me before, not in this realm. How the hell is this possible?

But Jeremy's inhuman growl drags me back to the nightmare.

"What the fuck did you do with Declan's body?" Jeremy snarls from the stage, his corrupted voice making my skin crawl.

I fight desperately to block out my familiar before he can respond, before he can damn us both.

But something inside me stirs.

That sadistic, chaotic nature that can't help but twist the knife deeper. That compulsive need to have the last word, to inflict maximum damage with surgical precision.

Declan Lovejoy won't reveal the truth to Jeremy. The truth is mine and mine alone—my weapon to wield against this broken creature.

My voice drops to something eerily calm, and I feel Lovejoy's horror spike through our connection. "It's killing you, isn't it, Jimbo? Not knowing what I did to him, where his body ended up? I bet you're dying to know every gory detail. How he begged for his life, how he screamed my name. I know you'd just love to wrap those grubby little hands around my throat and torture it all out of me."

Even as the words leave my mouth, a small voice in my head screams at me to stop. This is how I destroy everything. This is how I make every situation infinitely worse. I could walk away right now, leaving Jeremy to his corruption and Reagan to her power games.

But I've never been able to resist poking the bear.

"October, don't," Reagan warns, but it's too late. The twisted, insatiable claws of my sadistic impulses sink deeper into Jeremy, feeding my egomaniacal need to see him squirm.

"You know what the best part is?" I start, bending to meet him at eye level. "You'll spend an eternity wondering where it all went wrong, what you could have done differently, why poor Declan Lovejoy's legacy was crushed before it could begin. And here's what's truly delicious: you'll never see him again. Not in Heaven, that's for sure. Because that's not where I sent his soul, and that's certainly not where yours is headed."

Through gritted teeth, he snarls, "Where's. Your. Familiar?"

A predatory grin slashes my features. I press my left hand to my cheek, resting my elbow on my other arm, and bat my lashes. "Let's just say I traded my earring in for something more…*symbolic*."

That's when everything goes to Hell.

Starting with Lovejoy shattering my mental barriers like glass.

JEREMY! IT'S ME—DECLAN! SHE TRAPPED ME! I'M ALIVE BUT BOUND TO HER—DON'T LET HER WIN. KILL HER. KILL THEM ALL.

Fuck. *Fuck.*

The apprentice's demonic form convulses violently, ethereal light erupting from his eyes and veins, divine and infernal energies clashing within him. The air itself screams.

Jeremy's head snaps back, and a sound like reality tearing apart fills the club. Loud. All-encompassing. Suffocating.

White-hot energy explodes outward, consuming everything in its path. The walls buckle, the ceiling caves, and Hellfire meets holy light in a cataclysmic collision that reduces Bad Decisions to nothing but smoke and rubble.

Reagan and Cherry are hurled to opposite ends of the collapsing club—she frantically searches for a way to save her corrupted progeny while he desperately claws toward the exit. Cherry has no intention of protecting either of us. He's a desperate, disgusting weasel concerned only with his own survival.

We couldn't possibly be more alike.

When I spot the crimson clouds of Cherry's demonic teleportation swirling around him, something hardens in my chest. I'll never let him manipulate me again. Not me, not Reagan, not another fucking soul.

"Don't you fucking dare, you coward," I snarl at Cherry. I lunge for his pant leg, grabbing hold as his teleportation magic ignites, and within seconds, we're transported outside.

Into the brilliant California sunlight.

I scramble to my feet, brushing debris from my jacket, and mentally summon my Camaro. Within moments, she appears in all her candy-red glory, Mayhem waiting in the passenger seat exactly where I left him.

As I sprint toward the car, something wrenches at my chest—the urge to look back at my best friend, the beautiful red-haired demoness who showed me kindness and honesty during my darkest hours.

I made her what she is.

I destroyed everything for her.

And now, her life hangs in the balance because I couldn't keep my fucking mouth shut. Because I always have to have the last word.

I wouldn't blame her if she despised me forever. Fuck, I would.

But this is a battle I can't face. Not while the Night-mares and Fear Mark burns behind my eye, reminding me my immortal days are numbered once again.

I need to run. Find another Nephilim. Gather what allies I can.

The war between demon-kind is coming, and I am its catalyst.

The Debauchery Prime and his Underling watch their establishment explode into unholy flames. The devastation in her beautiful eyes is enough to shat-ter me.

Forgive me, Reagan. Someday, I'll make this right.

The cracked leather squeaks beneath me as I slide into the car. Mayhem, for once, says absolutely nothing and searches my ghost-white expression.

"Well, things just got a whole lot fucking worse." I sigh, shoulders tensing as I grip the steering wheel.

"Worse than what we dealt with Downstairs?"

"Much. Lots. Infinitely more." I glance in my rearview mirror, watching Bad Decisions burn to a crisp.

"Where's the Nephilim?"

I scoff. "He's not a Nephilim anymore. It was all a fucking ploy. I should have fucking known." I squeeze the scorpion ring off my finger and slam it into the glove compartment before sealing it with a spell. *Rot in there, you little shit.*

I look at my demon again. "We need to find another

one, but it's not safe for you. Not on this plane. You still want in? It's only going to get worse from here."

Mayhem grins, chaos glinting in those mismatched eyes. "If I wanted safe, I would've stayed at the Eighth gate, babe." He leans forward, that feral edge sharpening. "To Hell and back, October Winters. I'm with you."

There's something in his expression, something I can't place. A secret lingering, the ghost of his own fear and anxiety creeping through the chaos. He can't hide behind the kaleidoscope and void, not while his painfully human glamoured eyes tell me what's been so plain to see since the moment we met.

He is chaos. *We* are chaos.

We accept each other for our ugliest, dirtiest sides—sides others would destroy us for. Hell, some have already tried.

I've worked alone for a thousand years. I've never relied on anyone but myself. I don't need Mayhem. But fuck me, I *want* him. I want him to devour me whole.

In our darkness and corruption, we've found something eerily close to home.

A twin flame born of Hellfire and chaos.

We shouldn't make sense. We *don't* make sense. But we make each other better, and our best selves are everyone else's worst fucking nightmare.

He's more of a familiar to me than Lovejoy could ever be. Perhaps that was the Devil's plan all along.

My boot slams the accelerator, and the Camaro screams into the dawn, leaving nothing but exhaust, burnt rubber, and smoke in our wake.

To Hell and back.

Knowing me, I'll be there again soon enough.

EPILOGUE
INSANE IN THE BRAIN
WELL, THINGS JUST GOT A WHOLE LOT FUCKING WORSE.

MAYHEM

Neon lights flicker. On, off. On, off. Buzz, buzz, hum. Broken—always broken. Electric currents run through tubes like the chaos through my veins. Everything is so broken in this town. Broken buildings. Broken system. Broken hearts. Cherries everywhere. On every threshold, every corner. Red circle, red circle, stem. *Rotten.*

I hate it here, but I *love* it here. Flicker, flicker. On, off, on.

Focus, Mayhem. Stay in the fucking car. Be a good boy and keep it running. That's what you promised the Devil's Second when you kissed her. Beautiful, wicked lips. Cigarettes and leather. I taste her on my lips. I taste *her* on my lips. Sweet. *So sweet…*

Waiting. Always waiting. How long has it been now? No clocks in this old car. No watch on my wrist. Sun's not high enough to be midday. How long has she been in that club? She promised she'd be quick—witches are such liars, but this one is a beautiful, dangerous liar with a sharp tongue and sharper edges. I loved making her edges bleed…

Something is wrong.

Not *bad* wrong or *good* wrong, just…*wrong.*

Unbalanced, like my mind. Twisted. Groovy. Coming out of my head—not my head? *His* head. Spines. Two spines. Broken. Why does he have two spines?

The human realm is so upside down. Too *loud.* Too unstable. It makes me miss home, where everything is quiet and makes sense. I'm not okay up here—not okay, never okay. I can't control the chaos with so many humans ruining my playground. I am fucking starving. Need to eat. Need a snack. Need more secrets for breakfast.

Breathe, Mayhem. In and out. Focus.

Calm the chaos in your mind. Be human. *Be. Human.* Eyes shut. Deep breath. Pretend to be a human. Sit still.

She's fine. She can handle herself. She's *so* strong. Magnificent, deadly, and strong.

But why do I want to go in there so badly?

Car can stay warm without a body inside it. Have to get the kitten. *Meow.*

I hate this fucking place—but kitten loves it here. I

gotta love it for her. But nothing makes sense topside. It's too hot for a coat but too cold for a T-shirt. Human skin is useless. Glamours are wretched meat sacks. Kitten likes me this way. I like her every way.

Ditch the car and head toward the club. Right around the corner from the demon motel. Back door's here—*loved her back door, so tight, all mine*—just grab the doorknob and head on inside.

It's fine. Save the kitten. Do what the Devil said. Protect the Devil's Second.

Back door opens suddenly, a familiar face behind it. Old friend, old customer. Pretty Debauchery demon boy. Muscular—*beautiful* hair.

Charlie Maynard.

"Hey." Deep voice, shocked expression. Too close. Encroaching. "You're a long way from home."

"Maynard." I grin. Act normal. Be human. *Mask.* "Been a minute. Started to think you found another Chaos dealer."

Charlie looks over his shoulder, around and about, then back at me. He's hiding something. *Someone.* "Listen, Mayhem, I'd love to catch up, but I don't have a lot of time—I need you to do me a solid. Think you could spare me some of your blood?"

I rub my hands together. "Oooh, cooking up something new and exciting? Girls not wild enough at a strip club?"

"It's not for the club." That deep, spine-tingling

voice is a little too firm for my liking. "It's for…a friend. A vampire."

My head tilts. "Now what would a vampire need my blood for? Those fucks are crazy enough as is."

Charlie doesn't find my comment amusing. Too bad. "She needs to walk in the sun. Temporarily." Mmm, *she*. His jaw tightens. Worried. Desperate. So desperate, it smells like melted copper. "Chaos blood can rewrite physiology, right? Just for a few hours."

Red lights flash in my head—sirens screaming. Lovely, lovely noise. "Mmm, you sure that's a good idea, Maynard? Chaos blood in a vampire?" A grin splits my face. "She'll walk in the sun, yeah, but she'll also—well. You know. Side effects. Unpredictable side effects. Greed and Chaos in one body? That is one dangerous cocktail."

A delicious cocktail. Sin and tonic. Madness and hunger.

A muscle twitches in his jaw. "I'll take the risk."

"'Course you will." This is a terrible idea, which makes it a *great* idea. Kitten would love this—a chaotic Greed demon, a batshit vampire? They could be the *bestest* friends. We could *all* be friends. Maynard and his monster, and me with my evil witch. Just imagine all the blood, all the fucking, the fire, the mayhem. "I'll put it on your tab. You got a knife? Want it from the wrist? How 'bout the whole shebang—she can drink straight from my neck, make a whole show out of it. Bet she's a pretty one."

Charlie inhales sharply—mmm, hit a nerve there—and shakes his head. He reaches into his coat. "I got a bottle and claws."

"The gateway to every good time." I expose my wrist; Maynard shapeshifts his fingernails into claws and cuts into my skin. Which reminds me…

"You know, she's better off drinking your blood. Debauchery blood's perfect for shapeshifting. Less dangerous than my goods."

Charlie opens his mouth—to argue? To thank me?—but the words don't land, because—

Something shifts.

Not outside. *Inside.* Inside the club with the broken neon lights. *Inside where October is.*

The cogs and wheels turn inside my head. I wring out the last few droplets of blood into the neck of Charlie's bottle, and the spiral begins.

It's wrong. Something inside is *very wrong.*

Go inside. *Don't go inside.* When have you ever played by the rules? *Go the fuck inside.* Debauchery's a little cunt—no way he's going to let her walk out of there with what she needs.

Just go inside. Grab the kitten. Get the fuck out of here.

Not right. *None of it is right.* All a game—*whose* game?

Rook takes Queen. Checkmate.

Not right. Smells wrong. Tastes wrong—rotten, *rotten* Debauchery—GO INSIDE.

It starts with a laugh. A giggle, something small that turns into something bigger—uncontrollable. Maniacal. Inevitable. I can't contain the laughter. Everything is too much. Electricity through wires. Chaos through veins. It takes over like a beast in a frenzy. Magic pours off me. The human mask. The meat sack. A waterfall of electric, erratic energy pours from me until it finds its way inside Bad Decisions.

There's a loud bang inside the club.

No. October—*shit, shit, shit*. Got to get her. Got to protect her.

But she said she could handle it.

Another bang. Get out—get out—GET OUT!

My chaotic influence has fed the beast inside the club. Time. To. RUN.

"I need to get back in the car," I tell the pretty boy demon. "Don't be a stranger, Maynard." But Charlie Maynard is already gone with a bottle half full—half empty?—of my Chaos blood.

Last call for madness and Mayhem. Hope his pretty vampire survives the sun.

Blink. I'm in the car. Teleportation still works on the human plane—good, very good. The old Camaro roars to life without me touching anything, drives itself around the corner like it knows. Like it feels what's coming. Like she's calling for it.

Good car. Smart car. Smartest car.

And then, the whole club blows. Boom.

A broken building turns into a pile of rubble.

It was me.

It was my chaos. My influence. This is a stupid, unbalanced world where I'm a fish out of water, making everything worse.

I made things worse. I did that.

The passenger door flies open. October throws herself inside—no Nephilim with her; I fucking knew it. *Dirty, rotten Debauchery.* She's alive, breathing, covered in ash but alive. No burns. No blood. She got out. She's okay. *I haven't failed.*

"Well, things just got a whole lot fucking worse," says my little black cat. Such a beautiful kitten—so scared. The fears pour out of her in waves.

I made things worse. "Worse than what we dealt with Downstairs?"

"Much. Lots. Infinitely more." She sighs, and I want to drink in the chaos still spreading through her.

"Where's the Nephilim?"

She scoffs—what a pretty little sound. "He's not a Nephilim anymore. It was all a fucking ploy. I should have fucking known." She takes off her ring, shoving it into the glove compartment, and I'm seconds away from eating the little thing so she never has to face him again. Stupid little bu—*arachnid.*

"We need to find another one, but it's not safe for you. Not on this plane. You still want in? It's only going to get worse from here."

I want worse. I want everything bad and terrible—just as long as I'm by her side.

"If I wanted safe, I would've stayed in the Eighth gate, babe." The explosion still burns behind my eyes. The way the building came apart—*boom.* The way my chaos reached out and touched that holy-unholy monster inside and made it so much, lots, infinitely more worse.

She can't know. *She can never know.* "To Hell and back, October Winters. I'm with you."

Nightmares. Fear. Summer. Debauchery. Nephilim. Big explosions. Whatever we face, we will face it together. I will keep her deep, dark secret. I owe her that much. I owe her my immortal life, even if she never knows what I did.

Another secret I'll devour and take to the grave I'll never have.

Bury it deep, light the match, and never, ever tell.

READY FOR MORE?

The Hellion Harlot Collection (or Hellion-verse) is a multiple-book collection centered around October Winters and the badass ladies she meets along the way. Buckle up for thrilling, fast-paced novels, comics, and novellas welcoming you to the darker side of story-telling.

Be on the lookout for the third installment of the Hellion Harlot series, following **Indigo Moon** and **Charlie Maynard**. Running for their lives and haunted by their pasts, two demonic hearts bound by tragedy must survive an ancient evil—and each other.

From the mystical land of Los Angeles, California, Nikkita Bell is an author-illustrator who has carved out a distinctive niche where literature meets visual story-telling. Specializing in adult dark paranormal and urban fantasy with horror and romantic elements and a gothic neo-noir flair, each of Bell's novels become an immersive experience where readers encounter dangerous, high-stakes, and fast-paced narratives through captivating illustrations and music-inspired themes.

Through her groundbreaking hybrid graphic novel format, Bell welcomes you to the gothic side of story-telling filled with morally complex anti-heroines who embrace their darker natures and never apologize for it.

She has built her brand on a simple but powerful premise: villainous books about villainous women doing villainous things.

When she isn't crafting the next femme fatale to follow to Hell and back, Nikkita enjoys orchestral music, pretending to sing opera, and snuggling with her husband and two cats, Ciri and Yennefer.

Looking for more bookish updates, adventures, and kitty escapades? Follow Nikkita on Instagram, Tiktok, and Threads @nikkitabell, and don't forget to sign up for *The Hellion Harlot Club*, the Nikkita Bell newsletter, at nikkitabell.com!

Photo by Kitty Moffett of Missfitphoto.

DEMONIC GLOSSARY

Also referred to as 'The Big Thirteen' or 'The Primes,' the Thirteen Prime Evils are the head demons and sons of the Devil who have dominion over specific vices. Each Prime has Underlings that consist of High-Level, Mid-Level, Lesser, and Hellspawn (imps) minions that do their bidding throughout the human plane. Most demons live in their own level or realm in Hell, but a select few have a permanent foot on the human plane, where they may reign in a city or cities of their choosing.

DEMON OF CHAOS

This Prime is the embodiment of disorder, often manipulating and feeding off of human emotions and sowing confusion and disarray. Often appears as an unsettling, tumultuous, disjointed figure often compared to a swarm of bees. Chaos typically feeds on the aftermath of the events caused by majority of the demons, specifically Violence and Destruction.

DEMON OF DEBAUCHERY

Currently inhabiting Los Angeles, CA. Also known as Cherry (ala Debau*chery*). The master of excess, forbidden pleasures, desires, temptations, and indulgences. Occupies the seat of Hollywood, CA and the entertainment industry. Often appears in human form as an avant-garde, handsome young man in flashy clothing and accessories. Very colorful personality. Part of the Golden Trio (Deception, Debauchery, Greed).

DEMON OF DECEPTION

Currently inhabiting Las Vegas, NV, Deception is known as the 'cover up' or the 'cleaner' demon, Deception is typically in charge of protecting the exposure of the Underworld and supernatural creatures. He, along with Debauchery and Greed, have a permanent spot on the human plane and does not typically inhabit his realm of Hell. Deception is often associated with law enforcement (dirty cops), ponzy schemes, con-artists, thieves, etc. Underlings can take form of snakes, and primarily shapeshift and teleport in order to deceive. Typically causes unsolved murders. Part of the Golden Trio (Deception, Debauchery, Greed).

DEMON OF DESTRUCTION

One of the two oldest, most archaic demons on the list that isn't physically related to the Devil, and instead was an entity created by the forces nature and then given a corporeal and magical host through the Devil's power. The Demon of Destruction holds dominion over natural disasters (e.g. volcanic eruptions, tsunamis, hurricanes, earthquakes etc.) and is commonly worshipped by shamans and druids. Unlike Pestilence, this demon does take corporeal form and visits the human realm in the event of a large disaster occurrence and his form changes depending on the type of disaster. He specifically enjoys being in the thick of the disaster rather than sending Underlings to do it for him.

DEMON OF DOMINATION

Domination has played a bigger role in historical events and has manipulated the rise and fall of empires, monarchs, and kingdoms. Responsible for acts of slavery, brutal dictatorships, the implementation of caste systems, and royalty. While some believe that they were hand-chosen by God to lead nations, they were actually chosen by demonic intervention and manipulated through the power of this Prime. Rumor has it that he physically possessed history's most infamous humans.

DEMON OF DOUBT

Doubt is a shadowy presence that is not often seen in a corporeal form but is often seen on the human plane by other supernaturals (invisible to humans). He often invades human minds to sow paranoia, inadequacy, lack of faith, trust, and confidence. This demon is typically the cause of crippling anxiety and indecision, and often causes humans to be paralyzed by their own doubts. Often works hand-in-hand with Deception and the Fear and Nightmare twins.

DEMON OF ENVY

Similar to Debauchery, Envy is one of the more flamboyant and avant-garde Primes. Often the cause of one of the greatest sins of all, he is also depicted as immature and takes the form of a petulant child. He feeds on jealousy and resentment and turns admiration into hatred. He manipulates spite, covetousness, and his Underlings have the ability to steal the happiness from their victims.

DEMON OF GREED

Currently inhabiting Manhattan, NY, Greed is the typical money-grubbing Prime, Greed is the most intelligent and strategic of the 13. Often depicted as having dominion over politicians, financial institutions, and feeds on the desires of a human's pursuit of wealth. Greed acts as if he is better than the other Primes, and often pushes them around. He currently has a seat in Manhattan, NY and oversees major corporations and influences people of power. Part of the Golden Trio (Deception, Debauchery, Greed).

DEMON OF MISFORTUNE

Often referred to as the 'unlucky' demon or the 'bad luck charm,' Misfortune is the most recluse of the Primes, often keeping to his realm in Hell and using his Underlings to do his bidding on the human plane. He is the reason 'things randomly go wrong.' His Underlings take form of physical objects that act as bad luck charms and tethers him to the human plane without physically being on it. Typically worshipped by practicers of voodoo and hoodoo.

DEMONS OF NIGHTMARES AND FEAR

Also known as 'The Twins,' this demon is two in one body (therefore considered one solid entity despite their dominion over two evils). They often appear on the human plane in the form of the viewer's worst fear, but two headed. Their Underlings are best known for possessing children, and using them to do their bidding. When humans are asleep and being fed on by Nightmare Demons, they enter the Nightmare Realm in which they are vulnerable to soul consumption. Nightmare and Fear Feedings are usually what cause exhaustion, fatigue, and phobias in humans.

DEMON OF PESTILENCE

One of the two oldest, most archaic demons on the list that isn't physically related to the Devil, and instead was an entity created by the forces nature and then given a corporeal and magical host through the Devil's power. Responsible for sickness, diseases, and pandemics. Has not been seen on the human plane in centuries, but operates through his own realm in Hell and uses Underlings to spread maladies.

DEMON OF VENGEANCE

Manifests as a man who appears battle-weary with scars. He typically feeds off of humans' desire for revenge and turning justice into cruelty. He manipulates grudges, feuds, and retaliations. Often seen on the human realm working hand-in-hand with Violence, Envy, and Greed. He, himself, has a few feuds with his own brothers, and it is rumored that he does not favor Destruction and Pestilence due to their natural ties to the world rather than their sinful or emotional dominion.

DEMON OF VIOLENCE

The most powerful of the demons, Violence is known as the most ruthless of all the Primes. He is the cause of war, anger/rage, and physical and psychological harm. Of all the Primes, he has the largest army of Underlings at his disposal and he primarily operates from his realm in Hell. He is rarely seen on the human plane unless there is a mass world-wide event that he prefers to feed off of (WWI, WWII).

ACKNOWLEDGEMENTS

NIKITA, KRISTA, STEPHANIE, AND KATIE

I truly don't mean to rope you all together in one little paragraph, but my sentiments and love are the same for all four of you. I could not, and I mean COULD NOT have written this book without either of you. Months ago, the crazy idea of keeping this novella a secret came out of nowhere. At first, it was an idea born to protect me from burnout, but eventually, it turned into my first semi-surprise drop for my readers. I bugged each of you every single day, wondering if this was the right choice, if this story was worth telling, if writing a novella after just finishing Bad Decisions was even the smart thing to do, when book 3 was more important. The imposter syndrome bug hit hard. The "I want to quit" bug hit even harder. When I was dealing with the terrifying reality of possibly losing my sight, you four were there for me. You listened to my ideas and humored me with my crazy Mayhem antics. You all cheered me on, reminded me who I am, and told me to light the match in your own special ways. I love you all so very much.

Thank you for giving me the strength I lost and for being there for me every step of the way. Also, thank you for keeping this novella a secret with me. I imagine the day I finally announced it to the world was the day we all collectively sighed a breath of relief (No? Just me? Cool...)

SAM, MAGGIE, CJ, AND AURORA

To my beautiful dream team here, I love you all so very much. While some of you may have known what I was cooking all along, I always felt constantly supported by all four of you. You four hold a very special place in my heart, and have shown up for me in ways others wouldn't dare. I love our crazy group chats that FINALLY made it out of the chat back in March, and I hope will make it out again very soon. Thank you for dreaming with me, for giving the Hellion Harlots a reason to keep living and being bad, and for holding my hand on the dark days.

MARY CATHERINE

My beautiful lady. While the world was crumbling around me, you held my walls up. During the busiest convention season of my life, you reminded me to take a breath, eat a snack, and always try to be 5% better every time. I can't tell you how much you've saved me in the past few months. Thank you for being the backbone I needed when I needed it most, and thank you for believing in me when I couldn't. I love you so much.

JAYLA AND CHARLIE

Once again, here I go roping people into paragraphs, but I promise there's a method to my madness! You both were there the day I conceived Mayhem as a mere idea of a character. He was born of my undying love for Spencer Charnas, and not many people know that, but you both did, and you celebrated and supported my madness from the get-go. You may not know each other, but I will always hold you near and dear in my heart as the ones who helped me conceive Mayhem. NOW HE'S HERE!!!

CHERISH

My cheerleader, my sweet friend who always cries with me and laughs harder with me—thank you for helping me realize that I have my shit together way better than I think I do. Thank you for giving me the space to do what I need to do and ALWAYS honoring and respecting my wishes and trusting me to do the right thing. Your constant and unwavering support got me through the last few months, and I couldn't possibly thank you enough. And thank you for doing the first ever pass of the epilogue scene and helping me realize I am much better at writing ADHD than I ever expected. I love you so much!

KITTY

Even though you recently came into my life, you've made one of the strongest impacts. I am so grateful to have you as my older sister, who helped me get through this crazy season in life and cheered me on EVERY SINGLE DAY! Your support and love for my art is unmatched, and helps me feel like I'm doing something right every time. I love you so much!!

QUINN (SPECIFICALLY BAD INFLUENCE AND NAUDIO)

So, this is going to sound really dumb. Like, outrageously dumb. And will probably reveal way too much about my personal life, but here we go. When I started writing this novella, I was going through a really hard time. Physical, emotional, and medical changes all around. At some point during this trying period, I discovered the Quinn audio erotica app, specifically the voice actors/creators Bad Influence and Naudio. These two kept me going during the depression, anxiety, and days when I wanted to quit writing. Their immeasurable talent for writing and voice acting tickled my brain in a way I didn't think possible, and they were the driving force behind Mayhem's character and actions. Sorry, not sorry, totally stole (okay, borrowed?) 'kitten' from Bad Influence. I know these two will never see this, but I have to acknowledge them anyway. Without their weekly posts, I would have never found inspiration and joy in writing again during a depressive episode. Thanks for pulling me out of it, boys. Please don't stop creating content.

SPENCER CHARNAS

Another silly, outrageous one, but I need to take a second to include my favorite musician of all time here. Spencer is the lead singer of Ice Nine Kills, my favorite band in the world, and was the driving force behind my love for horror and the insane idea to create Mayhem's character. His vision and talent inspire me every single day to create, and I wrote A LOT of this book to "The Laugh Track," which is basically the anthem to Mayhem's character. Thank you for being the best, Spencer. I hope to meet you someday. By the way, Mayhem was modeled after you. LOL

HOUSE OF BELL (EDITING TEAM)

A million thank yous to Megan from Thorns & Roses Co, who squeezed this line edit in for me despite her crazy schedule and personal life, and loving Mayhem as much as I do (his spiky tail is thanks to you, babe). Thank you to Alexa and Sara, who have pulled through for me since Bombshell came out and will continue to be my shining stars. And especially Laura, the newest edition to my team, who absolutely blew me away with her incredible proofread! I am so lucky to have all of you. Thank you for helping make my babies the best they can be.

THE FABULOUS MR. BELL

I always save the best for last, but especially so for this book. You've always played such a pivotal role in my writing, but with this book in particular, you played the biggest role of all. You don't just support from the sidelines, you get on the track with me and race to the finish line by my side. I'll never forget the nights we spent workshopping Mayhem and Chaos' dialogue, ad-libbing some of the most ridiculous shit we could think of, only for me to go "wait a minute, that's fucking good, let me write it down." Mayhem and Chaos wouldn't even exist without you. You're as much their dad as I am their mom, just like with all of my work. You supported every late night, every early morning, and in the last few days leading up to production, you kept me sane and on track with everything. But most importantly… I dedicate this book to you. Because you're my chaos demon—the original chaos demon. I don't think many people in the world know what I mean when I say that, but we do, and that's what matters. In many ways, you are my Mayhem. You see every beautiful and ugly part of me, and instead of running, you bang your head against concrete till it bleeds. You celebrate everything that I am, and that's why I decided to immortalize you in this book, which I often call my therapy book. You're everything to me, and thank you for helping me light the match every time I find myself in darkness.